Candlelight
Ecstasy Romance®

"ALL RIGHT. YOU'VE JUST WON THE PAUL NEWMAN LOOK-ALIKE CONTEST. WHAT'S NEXT," SHE SAID.

Kathleen tossed her honey-blond hair nervously, unaware that her behavior was provocative.

"Next is the grandstand kiss," he said, and before she could voice an objection, she was enclosed in the strength of his arms, his lips crushing hers, showing his determination to steal her breath away. She gave a small gasp. Her hands turned into fists that rested on his chest, refusing to obey her orders. Instead, they slowly unclasped to move up the ruffled shirtfront and wind around his neck, her fingers losing themselves in the midnight darkness of his hair. Their long legs entwined as he leaned her against the railing, taking from her everything—everything she was willing to give. . . .

A CANDLELIGHT ECSTACY ROMANCE ®

WITH TIME AND TENDERNESS

Tira Lacy

A CANDLELIGHT ECSTASY ROMANCE ®

Published by
Dell Publishing Co., Inc.
1 Dag Hammarskjold Plaza
New York, New York 10017

Dell ® TM 681510, Dell Publishing Co., Inc.

Candlelight Ecstasy Romance®, 1,203,540, is a registered
trademark of Dell Publishing Co., Inc., New York, New
York.

ISBN: 0-440-19587-X

Printed in the United States of America

First printing—April 1983

To Linda Martinez, for everything

To Our Readers:

We have been delighted with your enthusiastic response to Candlelight Ecstasy Romances®, and we thank you for the interest you have shown in this exciting series.

In the upcoming months we will continue to present the distinctive sensuous love stories you have come to expect only from Ecstasy. We look forward to bringing you many more books from your favorite authors and also the very finest work from new authors of contemporary romantic fiction.

As always, we are striving to present the unique absorbing love stories that you enjoy most—books that are more than ordinary romance.

Your suggestions and comments are always welcome. Please write to us at the address below.

Sincerely,

The Editors
Candlelight Romances
1 Dag Hammarskjold Plaza
New York, New York 10017

CHAPTER ONE

Corrigan's Restaurant Supply was the best-dressed building on the block. Brilliant lights twinkled a cheery red and white. A deep-green canopy shielded the front entrance from the rain and snow and the posts were wrapped with wide candy-striped ribbon. Sitting on the canopy top was a giant jolly Santa, ho-ho-hoing toward a fake chimney. Bright wreaths of holly adorned with red and white polka-dotted bows were placed in the center of each window. But the final touch had been the tall illuminated candles on either side of the large glass double door proclaiming the entrance. Yes, Kathleen had done herself proud . . . again.

Achievement rated high in her book and this was the first year she had truly felt satisfied with both her public and personal life. Her personal life was just the way she wanted it—others may refer to it as boring, but it suited her to perfection. Her business life was a complete and total challenge that demanded all her energy.

With a jaunty step Kathleen walked through the large doors and turned toward the sign-in desk in the corner of the small front lobby, reaching for a pen even before she got there.

"Hi, José." she smiled at the dark, weathered man perched behind the desk, and he gave a toothy grin in return. He had been custodian here for as long as Kathleen remembered. Always friendly and very conscious of his responsibilities, José was in a trusted position.

"Gonna work late today, Miss Bolton?"

"No, I'll be through by this afternoon. The more paperwork I can get out of the way today, the more I can do Monday."

"I know what you mean. My wife says the same thing about housecleaning. The only thing is, there never does seem to be an end to it." He grinned again as he lifted the small gate that allowed Kathleen entrance into the main lobby of the five-story building. The tinkling sound of water splashing against metal told her that the fountains were still running. She turned the corner and passed the tall lush plants that shaded the center area. Benches of soft foam covered in forest green leather circled the fountain and lounge area. Small tables were scattered here and there with silver bells attached to the wood. They were used mostly at lunchtime when customers waited for the dining tables to be free. While waiting they could ring the bells for drinks to be delivered and thus ease the waiting time. Over to the right was one large glass wall separating the lounge area from the restaurant. Corrigan's not only sold to and supplied restaurants and hotels with their needs, they showed customers how it was best done with those two new facilities.

Kathleen had created the display areas and, as usual, her creativity and ambition had paid off. She was now vice-president in charge of sales, second only to the president, Ben Corrigan himself.

She walked quickly toward the glass elevators and punched the button marked FIVE. There was just too much to do on Monday not to try and get some of her paperwork done on Saturday. Besides, nothing was as important to her as her career.

The elevator whisked her to the fifth floor, silently opening to a wide, well-lit hall. She followed it down to her secretary's office, then farther in to her own private domain, only stopping when she reached her desk. She glanced around her office, still amazed and delighted that she had gotten this far in four short years. It felt good.

It had been wearing, tiring, and frustrating to compete against men in her quest for the top, but now she was content. She had come to work for Corrigan's with nothing more than a college degree, a pocketful of dreams and ideas, and a deep, silent need to plunge herself into activity. She had done what she set out to do. She had become a successful career woman.

Sitting down, she pulled the Wellington account file toward her and began working. She needed to check her amounts and quantities before she could send the completed account to billing.

In the middle of a row of numbers the phone rang, clanging shrilly in the quiet room. She reached toward it, a pencil in her mouth.

"Miss Bolton, here." She spoke absently, her mind still filled with figures.

"I thought you'd be there." Ben's voice rasped over the phone. From the slur of his words she could tell he was holding his usual cigar between his teeth. Kathleen could count on one hand the times when she had seen him without one, and it was usually directly after he put one out and just before he started on another.

"Hi, boss. What are you doing in on such a beautiful Saturday? I thought you'd be out on the golf course." It was his great love, coming a close second to his wife, Ellen, whom he had married over thirty years ago.

"You can't play eighteen holes when it's this close to Christmas, Kathleen," he mumbled through his cigar. "At least not in Denver. So I went to the driving range instead and hit a bucket of balls," he admitted with a chuckle. "And I thought I'd call and give you some good news."

Kathleen perked up. He had all her attention now. "Really? What is it?"

"You have an appointment on Tuesday to show the owner of the West Hotels what we can do for his restaurants." The pride in his voice was unmistakable. It was the largest chain of its kind in the country, with over seven hundred hotels in the northern

14

hemisphere, including the Bahamas and resort locations in South America and Canada. It was the coup of the year in the restaurant industry, and the only account Kathleen didn't want to touch.

"I'll tell you what, Ben. I'll set up the showroom and have the figures ready, but you take him through the hoops." She hoped her voice was calm, with just the right amount of indifference.

"What the hell do you mean? That's your job, not mine!" he bellowed in her ear. "I can't talk to those high and mighty types, you know that!"

"Any customer with as much clout as Stephen West deserves to have the president of the company give him the grand tour. He doesn't want to come all this way to be taken care of by a hireling." She modified her request, hoping it would work.

"Oh." Ben hesitated and Kathleen could almost see him chewing on his cigar as he mulled her words over. "I see what you mean, but, honey, you know you usually take care of the high-society types. And West is definitely in that class. He's a millionaire fifty times over," Ben stated dryly.

"He didn't get there by his own steam, Ben. It's all the work of his father and older brother, if I recall my newspaper stories correctly."

"It doesn't matter where he got his money. The fact that he wants to spread it around gets me excited. This account will put us at the top of the heap in the restaurant supply business. You know that."

"All right. I'll set it up for you." She could feel her pulse throbbing at the base of her temple. *Calm down, girl, calm down!* she told herself.

"If you really think I need to play the host, then I'll do it. I just don't want to look like a fool." Ben sounded unsure, and Kathleen knew he really didn't enjoy selling anymore. But he had to carry through with this. He had to for Kathleen's sake.

"Have I been so very wrong before?" She kept her voice light, but her hands were damp with perspiration.

"No, you seem to know that type well. You've brought in excellent business from that crowd of people. I can't understand them at all. They could be talking in another language for all I know. I can never understand the hidden meaning behind all the chatter." He snorted. "Garbage verbiage, that's what I call it."

"You'll do fine," she soothed.

"Right. See you Monday morning."

"Good-bye, Ben." Kathleen replaced the receiver quietly, her hand resting on it as if to maintain contact with another person. This wasn't the time to be alone. She needed to be busy so she wouldn't have time to think, or she'd wind up as tight as a toy guitar string.

Unbidden and against her will, Kathleen's thoughts flew back to the night of her college graduation over four years ago. Her roommate Sandy had invited her to a very special party.

"You've got to come with me, Kathleen." Sandy pleaded. "Every young son of a millionaire will be there, and I'm too nervous to face them by myself. Besides, you've met Claire and her older brother before. They were here just before Easter break. We met them at that small Italian restaurant just around the corner. And Steve gave you the sexiest eye all night long while you played coy."

"I wasn't playing coy." Kathleen defended herself, blushing with the thought of that night. They had talked and laughed and danced the entire evening as if they were two lovers alone in the world. His eyes, deep-set voice, even his hands, proclaimed more than words that she had all his attention and that he was pleased with what he saw and heard. His touch was heady wine, his voice brought out the stars on a cloudy night, and his eyes proclaimed her beautiful. Nothing like that had ever happened to her before. Kathleen had waltzed on air for a full week before she came crashing down to earth with the realization that he had never promised to call, never even asked her phone number. In time she realized he had thought of her as just another girl to flirt with to pass the time.

"Besides"—Sandy broke in—"Claire told me to ask anyone I wanted. And you're it."

"If her family's so rich, then what is she doing at this college? Why isn't she at Vassar or Brown or one like those?"

"Because her big brother thought that being among the masses might loosen her up a little. She's really very shy and timid. He thought she'd be eaten alive in a private university, while here she'd be ignored, at worst."

"But when Claire asked you to invite someone

17

else, I'm sure she meant another man, silly. Usually people date in pairs!" Kathleen chuckled.

"No. She said she had an overabundance of guys who want a chance to meet her brother and perhaps get their foot in the door of his business. She needs a few more females." Sandy sat back up, her eyes pleading. "Claire is rather shy and withdrawn but really nice. This is just her brother's way of helping her celebrate graduation with her friends." Sandy hesitated. "She told me he thought she should be more outgoing and this is his idea of fitting her into his mold."

"Sounds dreadful to me." Kathleen grimaced, but a small voice had already told her she was going. The thought of seeing Steve West again and verifying that he was really as handsome and conceited as she remembered was just too tempting.

"I don't get it!" Sandy wailed. "All year long you've been slaving away at the books, getting better grades than anyone I know. You hardly ever go out, look at the guys as if they have two heads while they drool all over you, and now you want to spend graduation night in this room?" Her voice squeaked.

Kathleen laughed out loud. "You're right. I should celebrate! Tonight I want all the wild, wonderful, wicked things that I never ever thought of before to happen to me. I'm going!"

"Good!" Sandy gave her a quick hug. "Now, what are you going to wear?" She stood and walked to their already crammed closets. "Something delicious and dreamy to go with that svelte, slim body of yours, no doubt."

18

"No doubt. Since the clothing I usually buy happens to fit my body," Kathleen stated dryly. "My mother thought it would look better that way."

Sandy chuckled. "You know what I mean! Everything you wear looks good on you. If I were tall, slim, and honey-blond, I'd have the guys all over me too. Especially if I had that invisible something called style."

"Yes." Kathleen's voice turned bitter. "You too can live in style on borrowed money and ill-spent time." She stood abruptly; the party mood had vanished. "I'm taking a shower. Back later." She left the room and headed for the bathroom. So much for tact, she told herself. She had always been careful not to mention her background or family, and now she had blown it.

As she stood under the steaming spray, Kathleen thought of her mother, working as a secretary for a law firm. She had worked ever since Kathleen's father had died of a heart attack two years ago. That was usually all the personal information she gave out. She never mentioned that her father had once been one of the wealthiest men in Colorado, or that he had been the single member of the family who should not have inherited. With his complete lack of business sense he had gone through a fortune and then some. Because of his bad investments, good times, and ability to ignore the inevitable, they had gone bankrupt.

The sloop Kathleen had loved, the cabin in the mountains close to the ski slopes, the large old English mansion they had lived in all their lives, money for her education, all were lost in a matter of weeks after her father's death.

Kathleen had been lucky in getting a loan to finish her education, leaving a top woman's university for a state-supported school, but her mother had had no choice but to earn her living. She had made quick strides in secretarial school and had worked her way up. Kathleen was proud of how her mother had adapted to her new, difficult responsibilities. But now Kathleen was graduating and would be able to return the favor of her mother's support and take care of her once more. She didn't want her mother working the rest of her life. It seemed to take too much out of her and she was growing slimmer and more pale every day. It was too late in her life to begin a new and highly challenging career, especially one she didn't want to begin with.

After the graduation ceremony Kathleen and Sandy headed for the West Hotel. Graduates were packing the roads, people hanging out windows, each congratulating the others. Everyone was buoyed high with the excitement of the hour and a reckless restlessness seemed to shimmer in the air. It was contagious. Tonight was a time for celebration.

The West Hotel was the city's most beautiful new attraction. The modern glass-encased skyscraper catered to the wealthy with discerning taste. Kathy laughed at some of the antics of the guys as they drove under the canopy ahead of her. It was hard to believe they were supposed to be the country's answer to the future.

"We've got a bumper crop of crazies in front of

us," she muttered, and Sandy chuckled, knowing what she was thinking.

"I know, but tonight is a special night. Can't you feel the magic in the air?" Sandy coaxed. "Tomorrow is time enough to be sedate and businesslike."

The ballroom was opulent, in golds and reds with a parquet floor that glistened in the muted chandelier light. Several tables of hors d'oeuvres were lined up on one side of the room while bartenders in crisp white jackets stood behind bars that marched along the outer wall. They mixed drinks with the dexterity that proclaims experience.

"Now, this is what I call a plush party!" Sandy whispered to her friend as they entered the double doors and stood in the receiving line.

"Sandy, I'm so glad you could make it!" Claire squeezed her friend's hand, her face bright with excitement. "You've met my brother Stephen. He's the one responsible for all this." She laughed gaily, but there was tension in the sound.

Kathleen's eyes darted around the room, deliberately keeping away from the man standing close to her hostess.

"Kathleen, thank you for coming." Claire's eyes openly admired her dress. It was a deep copper in color, with a halter neckline and a barely discernible slit running from hem to knee on one side. It set off her honey-blond hair and deep brown eyes, making her look like she just walked off the pages of *Vogue,* where the dress had first been seen.

She smiled at the girl's obvious sincerity. "It's

good to see you again, Claire. You have quite a party going on."

Kathleen's eyes flickered over to the dark, tuxedoed man standing next to her hostess, and her even breath caught, trapped in her throat as her brown eyes challenged his. Dark gray eyes stared back at her, a hint of amusement etched around his full, sensuous mouth. If his face had been on a bust in a museum, it would have attracted acclaim. His cheekbones were covered by taut tan skin, to form an almost perfect symmetry. A square jaw and creases on either side of his nose proclaimed stubbornness but also branded him with a sense of humor. But it wasn't just his features that were so outstanding. It was the energy, the strength, and the intensity that reached out to her.

He took her hand in his, caressing her palm with his thumb. "Hello, again." His eyes turned dark gray as he took in her appearance, noting with interest the natural peach flags of color on her cheeks. He watched her eyes darken with emotion to a chocolate tone and a smile tugged at his hidden dimples, exposing them for less than a moment before the look of boredom once more replaced the glint of interest he had first shown. It was as if the sun had hidden behind a dark cloud.

"It's nice to see you again, Mr. West," she stated primly, attempting to hold her dignity in place and wishing she could be swallowed up in the gleam of the parquet. She had never stared at a man before in her life and to be caught doing so was overwhelmingly embarrassing.

"My pleasure." His voice was deep and with just a hint of humor. She felt a tremor shiver down her spine. It sounded just like the tone he had used that night in the restaurant, a voice a man would use to best advantage as he whispered words of love into his woman's ear.

She retrieved her hand and escaped him quickly, accepting the first dance partner who approached her. They whirled around the floor, her eyes not seeing the young man who held her in his arms. She was lost to the image of Steve West looking down at her with that intense, indecent grin.

The strange feeling of recklessness that she had experienced earlier now took over her actions. Kathleen laughed, sipped wine, snacked, flirted, and danced with most of the men present. She was the life of the party and it soothed her ego to hear their outlandish praise, since she was being ignored by her host after his one intimate glance. She instinctively knew when he was near, doing duty dances around the now crowded room.. Whenever he came in her direction invisible vibrations seemed to stroke her skin. She didn't know whether it was by accident or design, but her eyes would lock with his, their combined glances speaking more than words could ever say.

"Isn't this the neatest party you've ever seen?" Sandy gushed much later, waving a cocktail napkin to cool her neck and face. She had been disco-dancing with a young man who seemed to put sparkles in her eyes and perspiration on her brow.

"It is nice," Kathleen concurred, suddenly feeling

like a slowly deflating balloon. For reasons she couldn't define, the very same people who gave Sandy such a lift were depressing her. "But I'm going back to the dorm now. I still have to pack and I'm already tired."

"I hope you can stand one more dance, Miss Bolton," a deep voice from behind her said, running pinpricks down her spine and telling her immediately to whom the voice belonged.

She turned slowly, her face blank, her lashes sooty against her now white skin. "I'm afraid I'm leaving, Mr. West. But thank you for the offer."

"Nonsense." He took the glass from her hand and gave it to Sandy. "Hold this, won't you?" His very best seduction smile made Sandy eagerly nod her head, her bright eyes wide as she watched him stare at Kathleen a long quiet moment before he took her in his arms and danced her onto the floor.

Kathleen could feel every vibrant inch of his lean body burning into hers, branding an indelible impression on her, and her face flamed at the thoughts that flew helter-skelter through her mind. He was too disturbingly attractive for her. She tried to pull away from the intimate contact of his body, but his grip didn't lessen. He ignored her struggle, continuing to dance. His closeness was causing her thoughts to swirl in chaos, his hands reminding her of his latent physical power. She had never been so affected by a man's nearness before, and it both frightened and intrigued her. Finally she gave in and molded to him, waiting for the music to stop and release her from his too close grip. But while she was here she would enjoy it, the little demon of recklessness told her. And she did, wrapping her arms around the strength of his neck, her head resting against the slick starchiness of his tuxedo shirt. When he felt her surrender, he pulled her even closer, a low sigh coming from deep in his throat and echoing in her ear. There were a thousand words that could have been spoken between them, but none sufficed for the moment. When the dance was over he sighed again.

"It's about time," he murmured seductively, tormenting her nerve endings with the smooth stroke of his voice and she involuntarily stiffened. He gave her a small squeeze and she relaxed slightly.

"What do you mean?"

"A little struggle for show is fine, but you don't have to keep it up for my sake. I'm on your side."

"Meaning this duty dance wasn't your idea?" she retorted quickly, ignoring the funny little prick of pain his words caused. "Well, congratulations on your extreme devotion to duty, but just for your information, Mr. West, I didn't want to dance with you either."

He grinned at her agitation and her heart did a somersault. "Calm down, lady. I was just telling you that you needn't go to any show of maidenly reluctance for me. We both know better, don't we?" He watched her face color with his insinuation and took it for guilt. "You've been staring at me all night."

"Only because you've been staring at me and I could feel it!" she cried defensivly. "Of all the insufferable, conceited . . ."

"Is there anything wrong with admiring a beautiful woman? At least it proves I'm normal." He teased her, completely unaffected by her anger.

"Or abnormal in your desire to embarrass me," she gritted through clenched teeth, trying once more to pull away from his lean body. She could feel every muscle move as he guided her around the floor, and it was exciting and dangerous. Much too dangerous.

"Stop wiggling before I do something you're not quite ready for," he commanded, and she quickly obeyed, knowing full well what he was talking about. "What you need is a breath of fresh air. All that wine must have muddled your thinking." So he knew she had been drinking wine! Slowly Steve danced her toward the large french doors at the end of the room. "Perhaps if I sober you up you'll realize just how much you want to dance with me. We make too attractive a couple not to continue this." The dimples were there, teasing her as much as his words.

They reached the balcony and Kathleen turned, gliding out of his arms and toward the railing before facing him again. The man was too virile for his own good and hers, and she had to defend herself from it.

"All right. You've just won the Paul Newman look-alike contest and I've just been pleasured to death by having danced with you. What's next?" She tossed her head in nervousness, swaying the honey-gold length of her hair over one slim shoulder, not really realizing her behavior was provocative.

"Next is the grandstand kiss," and before she could voice an objection she was enclosed in the strength of his arms, his lips crushing hers, showing his determination to steal her breath away. She gave

26

a small gasp and her hands turned into fists that rested on his chest, unable to do what she ordered. Instead they slowly unclasped to move up the ruffled shirtfront to wind around his neck, her fingers losing themselves in the midnight darkness of his hair. Their long legs entwined as he leaned her against the railing, taking from her everything she was willing to give. His lips turned into a gentler but more persistent pressure as he opened her mouth to seek and find the warm moistness within. He filled her with the scent and taste of him, and it felt right that he should. The gentle but insistent pressure of his hands roamed the length of her slim back and his touch brought a coil of molten fire alive deep down inside. Her head was spinning with the tender constancy of his touch, a slow but leisurely drugging of her senses. Everyday emotions were replaced by a wondrous submission as she gave into the myriad feelings that swamped her. She had never before reacted to a man the way she did him, and now her feeble mind couldn't begin to function properly, let alone instruct her limbs to pull away and stop the exquisite tortuous sensations he aroused. Without realizing it, her throat echoed a sound not unlike that of a stroked cat. Steve reluctantly pulled slightly away from her. Kathleen couldn't move. Her limbs had turned to rubber. Instead she rested her bent head against the hardness of his chest, afraid to see what was in his eyes. Surely he must know she had never surrendered like this before.

"Damn," he muttered thickly. "We started this too early, my Kathleen. So we'll just have to dance the evening away until the crowds leave and we can be alone together."

She nodded her head, not absorbing the words, just the tone of his softly muffled voice. He was as affected by her as she was by him! It was a heady thought to an already totally bemused Kathleen.

"I'm glad I had the foresight to get all those duty dances out of the way before tackling you." His throaty laugh sent chills down her spine.

"Did you do it on purpose?" she questioned softly, her eyes illuminated and starry from his kisses.

"Yes. I knew once I had you in my arms I would never want to let you go," he murmured, giving her pouting lips one more swift kiss. "And I was right."

After they entered the party room Steve once more took her in his arms. He molded her close to him, his breath teasing the strands of her hair and the small opening of her ear. Part of her reeled with the depth of feelings his hands could evoke while another part was amazed at her wholehearted response. He brought forth a yearning in her that she never knew existed until now. She floated on gossamer clouds, with him leading her from one puff to another. His body was always pressed close to hers, making her constantly aware of her own femininity. She didn't care who noticed that they were almost making love in the center of the room. She couldn't concentrate on anything except being in his arms. They spent the rest of the evening dancing, totally oblivious to everyone and everything. Once a couple stopped dancing and talked to them, but it was just an irritation and the people soon moved away, a knowing look on their faces.

Friends shouted good night and Kathleen waved back without really seeing them, her entire being concentrating only on the man who held her close, whispering outrageous, loving words in her ear. They chuckled together; they stole light kisses; they teased each other with sensations that couldn't be assuaged. Every time Steve looked at her his gray eyes would darken with an unknown message of promise, and she would glory in that look. She had been struck by lightning, and so had he.

The band played the last song and Steve took her in his arms once more, his grip tightening in ownership. She hadn't danced with anyone nor spoken to another man since Steve had taken her out to the balcony. And she didn't want to. This was the wonderful glow of love at first sight they had written songs about, and she reveled in it. Glancing over Steve's shoulder she could see more of the guests leaving and gave a sigh of relief. Once they left, Kathleen and Steve would be alone to say the things that needed saying and to revel in the feeling of finding someone to love.

Steve gripped her arm, almost marching her out to the balcony before bringing her back into the haven of his arms. She fit there so perfectly, as if she were meant to be there. His lips came down to claim hers in a kiss that was both tender and yet hungry with need. Kathleen answered it with her limited experience, telling Steve she was his, and he sighed heavily. He pulled back again to stare down at her, a glimmer of a smile about his lips as he leisurely toured her face in the moonlight. Her lips were swollen from his kiss, her eyes glazed with his lovemaking, her slender neck thrown back to invite the moistness of his lips. He didn't resist.

A wonderful lethargic feeling invaded her limbs, creating an immunity to everything except the touch of his firm hands and lips and the pressure of his body as he held her tightly against him. He held her up with his firmly muscled legs; her own were incapable of supporting her.

"I know you'd be like this the first time I saw you," he muttered, bending to tease the outer curl of her ear.

"Like what?" she whispered breathlessly, her head moving to keep in tender contact with his smoothly shaven cheek. His masculine scent mingled together with the night air, drugging her senses further.

"Like a goddess of love should be—warm, passionate, wonderful to love." He breathed deeply of her scent. "I promised myself I wouldn't see you after that night in the restaurant. I don't have time for complications right now. I need to tie up other loose ends first. But instead . . . here I am, making love to you just the way I wanted to, dreamed of.

"And am I a complication, Steve?" Her voice was husky with need and light with his sensuous touch, his fingers molding her skin. His words stroked over her as powerfully as his touch moved her. She had no feeling of right or wrong. It was perfect. They had reacted to each other from the very first time they met. She had always known it and apparently so had he.

"Yes. Heaven help me, you're a complication!" His breath warmed her temple. She reached up and grasped his head with her two hands and brought his mouth to hers to stop the flow of words. She had heard as much as she needed.

He took over, parting her lips even more, inviting himself into the sweet cavern of her mouth and exploring it deeply.

Finally he broke from her embrace. Taking her hand in his, Steve led her quickly from the darkened balcony and into even darker terrain. She followed wordlessly, trusting, still in stunned shock from the tremendous upheaval of emotions she had experienced in the past three hours. He stopped in front of another set of french doors and this time the room they entered was black as velvet, surrounding Kathleen in a cocoon of night. He pulled her just inside the room and quickly shut the doors behind him before bringing her into his arms once more, his fervent kisses stirring her to uncontrollable passion.

Somehow his jacket was shed and shirt undone and her hand was traveling the length of his matted chest. The darkness allowed her to see by touch, to act in a way that was totally alien to her. The evening's magic was all around her and the one she loved was by her side. A few minutes later and her halter straps were undone, allowing his lightly calloused hands the freedom of her tingling skin, his mouth wandering toward the sensitive cord between her neck and throat. Once more she was in ecstasy,

31

doing and saying things she had never done or said before, but which seemed so right and natural now.

He lazily stroked the silkiness of her back. "Slow down, my Kathleen, slow down. We don't want to finish before we start, do we?" His voice held just the right hint of intimate laughter and warmed her even more.

"You're very beautiful, you know." She followed his lead and nibbled on the lobe of his ear, breathing deeply of his musky shaving lotion.

A chuckle reverberated in his chest. Her honesty and eagerness were a refreshing aphrodisiac to his senses. "I'm supposed to be handsome. You're the beautiful one." As his hand reached down to the soft flesh of her inner thighs, the smoothness of her skin overwhelmed him. He took a deep breath and stilled his hands until he was once more in control. Once more his hands began traveling the satinlike skin, teasing her with a warmth and nearness that fed the ache in her.

She undulated against his hand, silently begging him to relieve her aching misery. In answer he pressed her back upon the couch they occupied, stretching out beside her as his mouth bent to tease a sensitive nipple, his tongue flicking it alive to send waves of heat through her already burning body. He molded her body to the thrusting urgency of his, gently pushing her here, pulling her there. She held on to his back, her nails digging into his muscled flesh as she swirled toward a destiny she did not know. Little rivers of fire flowed through her veins, heating from every point he touched. His lips searched her mouth for sweetness only to return to nibble and tease dusky cherry nipples into near bursting hardness. His hands were lightly skimming the secret sensitive parts of her, bringing her to a plateau she had never reached before. Then his hand was replaced with him, filling her, releasing her from earthly bounds and allowing her to float freely with him. Their bodies and breath synchronized for eons before gently floating down to earth.

In the space of a few hours a man she barely knew had made love to Kathleen for the first time in her life.

A small smile tugged at the corners of her mouth, but her musings were interrupted by Steve's abrupt movement as he left her side. He cursed under his breath as he reached for his shirt on the floor, stumbling in the moonlit darkness.

"Steve?" Silent tears slid down her cheeks, unbidden. She didn't know if they were tears of joy for what had just happened or tears of sorrow for losing what could never be replaced. But either way she was totally unprepared for his violence.

Rough hands reached out for her slim shoulders, grabbing and shaking her. "Why? Why would you go to bed with a man, let him take you, and not tell him it was your first time?"

"Does it matter?" she choked out, and he quickly let her go. She fell back to the hard cushions of the couch. Suddenly she felt dirty, used, and she saw the scene reenacted as others would see it.

Steve ran an agitated hand through his hair. He was sitting on the edge of the couch as far away from her as possible. "Yes! No! I don't know, damn it! But I should have been told. I didn't think there were any of your kind left in the world. It never even crossed my mind!" Then his head came up. Suddenly he turned and faced her, his eyes narrowing as he tried to read the expression on her face. "Or was that it?" he mused, as if to himself. "Were you trying to tie me up, little Kathleen? Were you saving yourself to snag a millionaire?"

Her breath stopped, eyes wide with hurt and disgust. "Is that what you think?"

"It's a definite possibility," he stated coldly. "You women are more devious than men could ever be."

She was chilled, and now that heated emotions had cooled, the facts clearly showed the sordidness of her actions. She stood and reached for her dress, not realizing her form was outlined against the moonlight flooding on the glass-paned door. She slipped it over her body with trembling hands, donning the garment as a soldier would wear armor. Her tears were dry now, and never, never again would they flow for what she had done tonight.

"Where do you think you're going?" He stopped her in mid-step as she headed quickly toward the large french doors.

"Home. To forget the mistake I just made. But first I'm going to take a shower and scrub the scent of you from my skin." She whipped around to face him in the dark room. Her chin lifted proudly and Steve could see the sheen of tears she now refused to let fall. "And don't worry, Mr. West. I realize you're out of my class, thank God! I'm not asking for anything from you. Consider it a gift!"

"You're not going anywhere until I get a few things straightened out," he growled, grabbing at her clenched hands as she turned to go. All evening long his touch had given her magical ecstasy, but now it brought sheer agony. She twisted her arm in an attempt to get away.

"No! There's nothing to discuss. I made a mistake! Let me go!" she cried.

His grip slowly slackened and he let her free. "You're right. Now isn't the time. But we're going to have a long talk tomorrow, Kathleen. I promise you," he said grimly.

"Oh, come now," she laughed, a tinge of hysteria in her voice. "Don't tell me you're going chivalrous now! Why don't you put on your bored act and hit another party. Perhaps next time you'll be able to pick up someone more experienced. Someone who knows the rules to your cruel games."

"Why, you little . . ." But she didn't stay to hear him finish his condemnation of her. She was out of the room quickly, slamming the door. She was oblivious to the glass shaking in the doorframe.

Within two hours she was packed and in her car, driving toward Colorado Springs. Toward home.

Never again would she see Steve West. Never. Her humiliation was complete and she wouldn't punish herself further.

Two weeks later she and her mother moved to Denver, and she began a new life and a new job with

35

Corrigan's. Then came four months of traumatic hell when she found herself pregnant with Steve's child. Explaining it to those who loved her, those she worked for, was hard enough. But when she lost the baby she had come to want desperately she thought she would never be happy again. It took her months to come out of her depression, but once she did she never looked back. But she never again had a relationship with a man. Once was enough.

Looking back, Steve West had actually done her a favor. Before meeting him she had thought all men were slightly silly. Now she knew she had been wrong. They weren't silly, they were dangerous and should be avoided like poison. No man alive would ever humiliate her again. Ever!

Stop! her brain screeched. The memories had flooded her, and with them had come the pain. Kathleen stood on trembling legs and walked slowly to the file cabinet. She had to forget Steve West and what he had done to her girlish dreams. She had to forget. She replaced the account she'd been working on and quietly shut the drawer. It was time to go home and relax.

Sunday Kathleen took a drive to shed some of the cobwebs she had accumulated overnight. Colorado was divided almost down the middle by the Rockies. To the east was farm country, plain flat land that stretched as far as the eye could see. The landscape was monotonous, spreading for miles without a single ridge or rise. It was just the view Kathleen needed as she sorted out her thoughts. There were no distractions.

Steve West. After four years a playboy like him wouldn't even remember the girl he'd made love to in a dark hotel room one night. There were probably too many before and after her. All she had to do was stay out of his way and the whole thing would be over in a matter of hours. Besides, even if he did remember, it was just as likely that he, too, would be embarrassed by the memories.

She smiled for the first time since Ben had called to give her the news. They were both older and wiser now, and those things didn't matter anymore.

Her mind worked furiously. She'd do the best display she's ever done. She imagined which china and silver to work up and what unusual china patterns she could show off to best advantage. She'd seen some new fabrics for tablecloths at the wholesaler's last week. One of them was a marbleized version of browns, tans, and white with just a touch of black. The pattern was dramatic and striking. Could she get the muted gold and green from another dealer? She thought so. The drive home was much quicker than the drive out, her mind buzzing with thoughts, ideas, color schemes. Everything would work out beautifully. It would!

Kathleen spent Monday morning working on her design. The day was busy and fast-paced and by the time it was over, Kathleen was bouyant but exhausted. She sat behind her desk, the figures she was working on blurring together. She could hear the muted calls of the staff echoing good nights to each other as they left for home.

Kathleen's secretary stuck her head in the door, obviously in a hurry to leave. "Anything else for tonight, Miss Bolton?" she called.

"That's it for now, Stella. Recoup your strength for tomorrow." Kathleen grinned, understanding the reason for the girl's haste. She had fresh makeup on and her dress was more formal than usual. "Got a date?"

"Yes." Stella was suddenly sheepish. "With Ron in sales." She waited for her boss to respond. It wasn't every day a secretary dated a bigwig in the company, let alone a man who used to take out the very beautiful female vice-president. "You don't date him anymore, do you Miss Bolton?"

"No, Stella," Kathleen reassured her. "But not because he isn't nice, because he is. Very."

"Well"—the younger girl was obviously relieved —"Good night, then."

"Good night."

The smile faded from Kathleen's face as the door closed. Ron had been a nice guy, congenial, pleasant to be with, everything that an up and coming man in business should be. But he wasn't her type at all. She leaned back and sighed. No one was her type, at least no one that she had ever met. And she wanted to keep it that way. She was happy as she was.

Ben gave an impatient tap on her door, his usually merry brown eyes showing concern.

"You've been going full swing all day, Kathleen.

38

Don't you think you should call it quits for now? You still have tomorrow to work, you know."

She ignored his question. "What time is Mr. West due to grace you with his presence?" she questioned, her nerves disguised with sarcasm.

"At one o'clock sharp."

"Has he taken any other bids on this job? I'd like to know the competition. If my figures are correct, this will be the biggest job Corrigan's has ever had."

"I'm not sure, but if I had to guess I'd say he also contacted Spencer's Supply in New York. It's our only competition."

"And they'd cut prices just to eliminate us from the market." Kathleen leaned back and closed her eyes, shutting out the late evening rays of the sun. "The cloth sample I ordered is absolutely dynamite. All the other tables are set and ready to show."

Ben walked over to the file cabinet, pulling out the bottom drawer and extracting a bottle of Scotch he kept there for just such an occasion as this. He wasn't a heavy drinker but enjoyed a shot after a particularly busy day. And since he was always the first to leave, he usually stopped by Kathleen's office to check the day's business. He took two small glasses from a sample dining table sitting in the corner of her office, then poured himself a hefty amount and Kathleen a much smaller portion. Passing it to her silently, he sipped on his, then watched her cautiously wet her lips. It was Ben's favorite drink, not hers. But she was lucky to have a job like this and work for a considerate man like Ben. She was lucky . . .

"Thanks, Ben," she stated simply, taking another sip.

He peered over his bifocals to take in the tired lines around her eyes and mouth. The girl was pushing herself too hard. He didn't know whether to praise her or scold her. Certainly his business had doubled since he had taken a chance and hired her. She'd been green and full of eagerness. And the new accounts had all been her own doing. He was too old to aspire to the top of the heap. As long as he had a good income, and it was more than enough, and time off occasionally to play a little golf, he was happy. But Kathleen kept going even after the money was there, the bonuses were paid, and the business was done.

In a way she made him feel old, for he could remember the days when he had been driven by the unseen ghosts of ambition. But when he'd almost lost his wife to surgery, everything fell into perspective. Ellen came first and everything else came second.

"You work too hard," Ben mumbled. "You should slow down. You act as if you want to buy me out before you reach thirty."

She laughed, a low sound that played sweetly on his ears. "I work because I enjoy it, Ben. Your company has been just what the doctor ordered," she confessed, a twinkle showing in her light brown eyes. "Besides, there's a new challenge every day. What more could a person ask for?"

"A home, family, children to keep you occupied, a husband to make you happy." He watched her face turn white, knowing he had hit a nerve with a scatter

40

gun. He didn't know which thought frightened her more.

"I have a home, my mother is my family, and I certainly don't need a man to keep me happy. A person can't rely on being kept happy unless it's within themselves," she stated softly. "Besides, I have Corrigan's"

"And children?" he persisted, watching the expression on her face close like a dying flower. He remembered when she had first come to work for him she had been pregnant and barely able to look anyone straight in the eye. But slowly, as he'd drawn her out little by little, he had realized just how quick and alert she was to the problems concerning his business. He had hired her against his better judgment, had tested her over and over again but never found her wanting. Even when she had lost the child.

"You know how I wanted that baby, Ben, but now I know that what I'm doing right now is far more satisfying than anything else I've ever done." *And less emotional or hurting,* she thought bitterly.

"Does that mean you want to help Mr. West with his selections tomorrow after all?" Ben teased, trying to bring her smile back. He was a fool to push when he should have pulled.

"No." She swallowed the rest of her scotch and stood, reaching for her purse in the bottom drawer. "It means that everything will be set up for you to handle while I work on the Main Linen account." She hid the denial with a smile. "And now I think I'm going home to get a good night's sleep before facing that virago of a seamstress tomorrow. She

41

threatened to leave if I provide her with one more surprise on the eve of a showing."

Ben's good-bye echoed in the now quiet office. She walked toward the door, listening to the hollow sound her footsteps made, trying to ignore Ben's words. But they continued to resound in the empty hall. *Children to keep you occupied, a husband to make you happy,* he had said, not realizing that those words would produce a stabbing pain in the pit of her stomach and bring bright tears to her eyes.

She paused in the giant parking lot and watched the traffic slowly moving out of town and toward the suburbs. Everyone was eager to get home to their families.

Kathleen had turned Corrigan's into her children, her husband, her lover, giving it every ounce of love and care she would have given a family. She opened the car door with a jerk, angry with herself. Well, so what? Wasn't that what she wanted? Wasn't that what her father's death had taught her? Never slide along in life when you can control your own destiny. Only a fool allowed circumstances to mold his life, and only a fool would trustingly give love to another.

The house was empty. A note on the kitchen table stated that her mother was out for the evening and there was a casserole in the refrigerator. All she had to do was heat it in the microwave.

Suddenly her eyes glittered with determination. No leftovers tonight. She'd treat herself to dinner in one of the finest restaurants, where people would be gathering to talk and laugh and dine in style. Why not? She made more than enough money to pay for whatever she wanted, why shouldn't she splurge a little? Everyone else did.

Within an hour she had showered and put on a new slate gray dress she had been saving for a special occasion. And this seemed to be it. Glancing in the mirror, Kathleen was pleased with herself. The dress had a deep V neckline that showed off the slender column of her throat to perfection. She gathered her hair and twisted it into a smooth coil at the base of her neck. Suddenly she was relaxed and eager to eat. Within minutes she was in her car and on the highway, heading for one of the more exclusive steak houses in the city. A song came on the radio and she grinned. The lyrics told her to do herself a favor.

Within another twenty minutes she was seated at a table for two. It was directly against a window, overlooking a small interior atrium. It was a beautifully serene scene complete with a small creek and an arched wooden bridge crossing it.

The service was impeccable, the food delicious. She lingered over a coffee liqueur, enjoying the view of the garden and the quiet dignified atmosphere of the restaurant.

Then something made her alert and she glanced up to look around, the soft skin on the back of her neck prickling. Several times this evening she had had the feeling that someone was staring at her, but each time she looked around there was no one there. Her nerves must be stretched more tautly than she'd thought. Perhaps she should slow down a little. She wasn't usually in the habit of imagining things.

She quickly paid her bill with a credit card, then

43

stood to leave. As she pushed her chair under the table the sensation of someone staring at her was so strong she turned, only to gaze into the smoky gray eyes of the dark-haired man seated directly behind her. Her face whitened in the dimly lit room as she recognized him. The shock of seeing him was an almost tangible thing that shot through the air between them. His eyes darkened under a thundercloud brow that could have cooled the Arctic as he virtually raked her slim body from head to toe, raping her with his eyes. A shudder ran down her spine, making her hands tremble and legs shake. He gave a nod as if dismissing her from his mind and view, then turned back to the beautiful brunette seated across from him, turning on a smile that would have melted the very same continent he had just frozen moments earlier.

Kathleen didn't know how she got from her seat to the car, but she did. It took her several more shaky minutes to be able to drive away.

Why? Why did he have to intrude upon her now, after four years? She didn't have an answer. All she knew was Stephen West was back, and this time her reaction to him was more devastating than ever. He had turned her calm competency into a mass of quivering jelly.

Damn him!

Damn Stephen West!

CHAPTER TWO

Kathleen spent a restless night, her dreams replaying pictures of Steve as he was in the restaurant that night—cold, ruthless, the epitome of the handsome playboy filled with the thirst for excitement that could only become more jaded as time progressed.

She remembered those terrible first few months after her graduation. She had been terrified. Terrified that he would find her and just as terrified that he wouldn't. But she need not have worried, for he never tried. Once in a moment of panicked weakness she had called his family home in Florida, asking to speak with him. Her voice had quivered with barely controlled emotions, so tight and squeaky that they had to ask twice whom she was calling. After a moment his older brother came to the phone. His voice sounded so much like Steve's that she clutched the telephone even tighter, her stomach clenching in reaction.

His voice was weary at the interruption. "He's not here, as usual," he stated. "If I were you, honey, I'd forget him."

His own bitterness came through loud and clear, confirming all of Kathleen's worst doubts. She had heard the rumors about Steve, had read the gossip columns and seen the magazine articles concerning his love affairs and globe-trotting trips with luscious, sophisticated women at his side. He was the playboy of the elite. The one man every other man wished he could be. He used women like other men used ties, discarding one at the same moment he chose another. No one knew that better than she.

The shock of tumbling immediately into bed with the first man who'd burst through her barriers coupled with her guilt over the very actions she had always so easily condemned in others had made her encounter with Steve especially traumatic. Freewheeling sex had always seemed shabby to her, then suddenly she was hanging by her own censorious noose.

Thoughts of Steve had her tossing and turning all night long. Finally toward morning she slept a deep and dreamless sleep.

Tuesday morning was filled with slushy rain. It dripped from the eaves, shined the sidewalks, and held the dreary dampness in the air.

The office was a beehive of activity. The young secretaries, alerted to the imminent arrival of the

46

famous playboy, Stephen West, were in a constant dither. No one wanted to be caught not looking her best, so mirrors were checked and rechecked.

Kathleen glanced into the showroom, pleased with what she had done. The room shone with bright crystal and sparkling plates. Each of the twelve tables were set to perfection, a showcase for the varied patterns and designs. She had indeed outdone herself.

A quick glance at her watch told her it was time for the great man to arrive and, straightening one last napkin in its holder, she quickly walked out the door and into her own private office. She didn't want to be anywhere near the vicinity of the showroom when the stormy gray-eyed man appeared. He had caused her enough heartache. She smiled bitterly. It was about time he paid off, even if the payment went to Corrigan's.

She forced herself to concentrate on the columns of figures in front of her, knowing she wouldn't really get anything done until Steve West left.

The minutes ticked by slowly. She leaned back and rubbed a hand over her forehead, willing the tension out of her body. Christmas carols wafted over the P.A. system and she closed her eyes, listening to the music, hoping it would wash away some of the tired depression she was feeling. Slowly the muscles that cramped her neck and back relaxed and she gave a small sigh as she leaned her head all the way back to stretch and untie her strained nerves. Soon he would be gone.

Two sharp knocks, Ben's signal, and her door

opened farther. Not waiting for an answering call, Ben ushered in his prize, pride making the older man strut like an oversized peacock. He had just done business with the best.

Kathleen rose slowly, placing her hand on the top of her desk to stop the slight shaking. She looked calm, composed, even though she was meeting the man she hated more than she'd ever hated anyone. Somehow she wasn't surprised to see him. In fact, down deep inside, she had expected this. Steve stood just inside the door, returning her cool look with a more intimate one of his own.

He was still the handsome man in the tuxedo; broad shoulders, lean hips, midnight black hair that shone with health. But his life-style during the past four years had left its mark so he looked even more handsome . . . and more jaded. His stance was casual on the surface, but the pantherish tightening of his steellike muscles were there, cloaked by civilized standards. His arrogant look confirmed her evaluation as they raked her body from hips to carelessly brushed blond hair.

Her chin rose and she dimpled her cheeks with a smile that didn't quite reach her eyes. "Hello, Ben." She inclined her head toward the guest. "Hello, Mr. West."

"Mr. West was so impressed with the display that he asked to meet the person in charge. I brought him right to you so he could applaud you personally." Ben gave a conspiratorial wink before turning to show his guest the large leather chair at the corner of the desk.

But before he sat down Steve's hand was out, spanning the desk as he waited for her to offer hers. Slowly she raised her hand and placed it in his. Old feelings swamped her as his touch ignited emotions deep inside. His thumb seemed to caress the top of her slight fingers, his touch searing through her like wildfire. When he finally released her she grabbed one hand with the other, rubbing it as if to erase the imprint of his flesh. He watched her and smiled.

Steve sat down, his steel gray eyes holding hers. His expression was implacable, and she knew that he could tell how much she had hoped to avoid this meeting. And he was laughing at her! Kathleen kept her anger controlled, however, and she spoke in a surprisingly even voice.

"I'm pleased you liked our display."

"And I'm pleased that you're pleased." My God, he was mocking her! She glared into his eyes, almost hypnotized by his stare. His searing look never drifted from her face.

Ben cleared this throat and tried to bring the conversation back into line. "Mr. West has chosen two or three for consideration, Kathleen. He has wonderful taste. He picked the very same ones I would have chosen, including the new table you just finished. It was the most striking setting on the show floor."

She tried to paste a smile on her stiff face. "Thank you," she murmured before locking her even gaze with Steve's. If he wanted to butt heads together, she was only too willing. "And what others are you interested in, Mr. West?"

This was impossible! She should have told Ben she

didn't want to see this man! But the telling would have led to an explanation and she knew she couldn't have handled that. She was having a tough enough time holding on to her facade of sophisticated coolness without Ben knowing their real relationship.

Steve gave Kathleen the numbers of the tables without consulting the small pocket secretary in his hand, his gaze continuing to devour her face. She raised one eyebrow in amusement at his childish tactics, hoping a blush wouldn't tinge her cheeks. He was trying to embarrass her into losing her composure. *Two can play at your little game, Mr. West,* she thought, *and I've had plenty of practice in the past four years.*

"Tables three, four, and twelve were the most bright and original." His voice was calm and eventoned, but the message was still there. He made it seem as if he were whispering sweet nothings in her ear, flattering her before taking advantage. Not again. Not ever again.

"That's high praise indeed coming from someone as *experienced* as yourself," she stated sarcastically. When she saw the smile on his face she realized just how much of her anger she had given away. Damn that man!

Ben's expression was one of surprise mingled with puzzlement. She had never before talked to a customer that way. "But surely you want your restaurants to look the same. Didn't one setting stand out from all the rest?"

"Yes, if this were being done for my restaurants. But that's the final prize, Miss Bolton. The testing comes first." His next words brought her sitting up straight with a snap. "I'm opening a new dimension in polo centers, similar to the concept of golf courses with homes and condominiums surrounding the play areas. I need each of the twenty-four cottages completely outfitted with kitchen equipment and accessories. And I need it done quickly."

The room echoed in silence. Surprise was written all over Kathleen's face, showing the shock his words had been.

A polo center! She should have known the playboy that was present four years ago was still present today. But disappointment was there just the same. If her expression mirrored her thoughts, Steve took no notice of it as he continued.

"Each kitchen has a different color scheme and I want each to match or blend with the individual cottage."

"Don't you think that's the job of a decorator instead of a restaurant supply house?" Her heartbeat quickened. There was a foul smell to this whole setup. She just wasn't sure what it was.

"If I wanted only the cottage kitchens decorated, then you'd be right. I wouldn't need you," he stated blandly, firing Kathleen's temper with his easy dismissal. "But I'm able to kill two birds with one stone this way. I must have the restaurants in my hotels refurbished, and it must be done by a reputable firm. What better way than to try you out than on simple cottage kitchens?"

"You're using the cottages as a training ground?" Her anger was barely under control. At his nod she continued. "You do realize the cost of such an endeavor would be extremely high. Everything would have to be ordered in ones and twos and that would drive the price up considerably. You'd be better off choosing a neutral scheme and buying in bulk."

His gray eyes narrowed, trying not to show the flash of irritation there. A rippling sensation of fear flowed through her neck to disappear into her toes, but she wouldn't let him know for the world just how that look had affected her.

"I've never had a problem paying my bills before. What would make you assume I would begin having that trouble now?"

A faint blush colored her cheeks and her mouth tightened in anger. "I'm sure you won't, Mr. West. Not with West Corporation's money behind you." Damn! She should't allow him to see her anger!

Ben glanced quickly between the two, realizing the conversation was heading for trouble and not quite sure how to avoid it. "Kathleen didn't mean to imply you couldn't afford our services. She was only pointing out the disadvantages of buying singly rather than in bulk."

"And it's a point well taken," Steve stated smoothly. "But I've already spent a fortune to get the club the way I want it. I see no reason to skimp now."

"I see." Kathleen glanced down at her hands in her lap. They were clenched tight and she had to force herself to relax them. "In that case, if you'll send us the color schemes of the kitchens, I'm sure you'll be more than satisfied with our work."

"No." Steve's voice was soft but with the implacability of a stone wall. "I don't want this done with long-distance colors. I need someone to spend a week or more going over each cottage, planning and combining the accessories each needs. Doing it by long distance could well have you buying orange thingamabobs instead of cranberry."

"Then perhaps we could work through your decorator," she persisted.

His eyes became narrow slits, his smile without humor. "I didn't know Corrigan's was so averse to money." He placed his hands on the arms of the chair, preparing to stand. "Perhaps I'd better try your competition, Spencer's."

Ben's head had been going back and forth, like a judge watching a tennis match. But now was the time to step in. Spencer's was his only competition, and pride alone wouldn't allow Ben to send a customer to them. Especially one this size!

"Just a moment, Mr. West. I'd like to discuss this with Kathleen. I don't see any reason why we can't come to an equitable agreement on this, do you?" He smiled the words and Kathleen felt rather than saw Steve's arm muscles relax.

"Certainly not."

Just then her secretary stuck her head in the door. "Mr. Corrigan? Mr. Madison is on line three for you." She gulped, still obviously intimidated by the millionaire sitting across from her boss.

Ben chewed on his cigar for a moment. "I'll take it in my office, Stella," Ben decided, then turned toward his guest. "I'll be right back."

Steve nodded. "I'm sure I'm in capable hands,

Ben." His eyes traveled the length of Kathleen's secretary, and she gave him a wide, sexy smile in return. Frustrated anger boiled in Kathleen's stomach. He certainly knew what some women wanted. But not her. Definitely not her! Once again her hands clenched together under the shadow of the desk.

Suddenly Ben was gone and the door closed silently behind Stella. The room was oppressively quiet. Her eyes darted to Steve's implacable face, only to find him staring at her, a slight frown of puzzlement on his brow. "You've changed, Kathleen." His voice was soft, sensuous, scraping against her taut nerves.

"But you haven't, Mr. West."

He leaned back in his seat, obviously set to enjoy the next few minutes of privacy. "Ah, but you wouldn't know, Kathleen. You only saw the icing without tasting the flavor of the cake."

"I didn't need to know the flavor. The icing was enough to make me sick," she shot back, disregarding previous thoughts of keeping her temper under control. "Besides, I'm surprised you even remembered one night out of so many."

His hands were relaxed on the arms of the chair, his legs crossed casually one over the other. He looked like the perfect ad for good liquor, damn him! She ignored the fast pace of her heartbeat and the clamminess of her palms, allowing only the disdain of her expression to show.

"Oh, I remembered," he stated softly. "Who wouldn't remember the girl who gave herself as a beautifully wrapped gift and then ran out into the night, never to be found again?"

"Never to be found, or never to be looked for?" She wanted to bite her tongue as soon as she said the words, but it was too late.

"Oh, I looked. I called your roommate the next morning, but she couldn't remember her own name let alone where you had gone." A sadness of the memory touched his face. "I tried to find you, but a family emergency arose and everything personal had to be shelved." He leaned forward in his seat, his gray eyes turning almost black as they seared through her. "And did you want me to find you, my Kathleen?"

His idea of an apology came four years too late. There would be no quarter given. "I wanted you dead, if you must know."

A muscle twitched on the side of his jaw, and he leaned back once more. "I don't think you knew what you wanted, Kathleen. Especially then. You were too young to be allowed out at night by yourself, let alone at a party like that one."

"I am not *your* Kathleen!" she gritted. "In fact, you may call me Miss Bolton."

"Still vitriolic?" His voice was velvety smooth and low-keyed with just a hint of laughter. "You'll always be my Kathleen."

"And you'll always be a playboy! What's the matter, Steve? Did all the women finally bore you to death? Is that why you're building this new polo club? Another toy for a millionaire?" Her voice built, but she didn't care. "You couldn't find anything in the world that would be worthwhile for you, so you're trying new playtoys?" She rushed on, not caring. Four years of bitterness were finally exploding inside her. "I hate people like you. You think you can buy anything, do anything, and it's all excused because your rich!"

"Do you feel better for having gotten that off your chest?"

"Nothing would make me feel better unless it was watching your back as you leave my office. I work for a living, and you're taking up my time."

"Everything you've just said sounds more like jealousy than hate, my Kathleen."

She stood, reacting to his words as if a whip flicked her skin. Her face turned white, but no words poured from her mouth; they all buzzed around in her head, making a droning sound. Steve, too, stood, facing her across the desk.

"Where's your femininity? You've lost that vulnerability that first touched me so." He mused aloud. "And it isn't because you've been in business too long. I know many women in business who didn't sacrifice their membership in the fair sex." He stared at her, bemused at the softness of her features. "Do you miss a man's arms, my Kathleen? Is that what's wrong? Do you miss kisses and caresses, arms around you, holding you, showing you what love is all about? Is that what's wrong with you?"

"I miss your absence!" she gritted, holding her breath before her heart pounded right out of her mouth.

He leaned over the desk, and although she knew what was going to happen, Kathleen couldn't have moved for the world.

"Then in my absence, miss this!"

His hand clasped the back of her neck as his lips clamped on hers, showing the depth of his anger. Her lips felt bruised and she could taste the bittersweet saltiness of her own blood. Her head whirled, stars showering her closed lids as he continued to batter her mouth with his, not softening until she capitulated. Then, slowly, he became tender, the pressure of his lips seeking, finding the response he was looking for. His tongue wandered through her entire mouth, plundering, drawing, easing, teasing. Bit by bit he drained her of resistance, leaving nothing but a deep need that flowed quickly through her veins to cry for more. His hair was crisp and curly under her hands and his touch burned through the soft skin on her neck to pound in her temples and at the base of her throat. His thumb touched the silken hollow where it pulsed, massaging the vein only to have the pulse beat faster, quickening in desire.

"It seems you missed me more than you care to admit, my Kathleen. No one has a reaction like that unless they care." His voice was sandpaper-rough and slightly foggy, exposing the depth of his own disturbed emotions.

"Go to hell, Mr. West."

Ben walked back into the room, his jolly face wreathed in a smile. "I'm sorry to have kept you both waiting, but business is business." He grinned before noticing the heavy silence. He glanced from Kathleen to Steve, noting the tightness, the visible tension between them.

"And now, Steve, I'd like to take you downstairs

57

to have a drink in our own bar. I don't know if you noticed, but it's another of Kathleen's ideas that has certainly paid off for Corrigan's." He rambled on, drawing Steve's attention away from Kathleen. She slowly sank back into her seat, thankful that Ben had intervened when he did. Her legs were weak and her mind a complete blank.

Both men were walking to the door. Then Steve turned, a wicked glint in his dark gray eyes. "It was ... interesting meeting you, Miss Bolton," he stated formally. "I'm sure we'll meet again."

"Really, Mr. West?" she dismissed him from her doorway, not allowing her body to shake with nerves until the click of the lock confirmed their leaving. Then she buried her face in her hands, trembling inside with the reaction of seeing Steve again. Nothing had changed. She was older, and smarter, and should have known better, but he still affected her the same way he did four years ago. Would she never learn? Could she really be so dumb and naive as to react to his kisses as if he meant them? Apparently so.

She took a deep breath, forcibly calming her pulse down until it was at a reasonable level once more. She had to be composed when Ben came back and demanded an explanation for her behavior. But how could she explain that Steve West was absolutely immoral, contemptible, and someone she couldn't deal with? She should have told Ben that she had known Steve before, but now it was too late. Both she and Steve had played the charade through in front of Ben and now they were cast in their roles. However,

Ben wouldn't stand still for her rude actions today. And she didn't blame him. Under normal circumstances she wouldn't stand for it either.

Usual was the key word. To her boss everything had been usual except her behavior. A customer had a legitimate business request and she had been rude. What could she tell him? That she had met that playboy one night four years ago and after a brief four-hour affair had been totally humiliated by him? No. Even to her mind that sounded incomprehensible. Hell hath no fury like a woman scorned, only she hadn't been scorned, she'd been devastated. And that feeling was just as strong today as it had been then.

"Would you explain what the hell is going on here?" Ben muttered through his teeth as he bit the end of his smoldering cigar. He plopped down in the chair he had recently vacated and squinted his eyes against his own smoke. "I've never seen you like that before. Usually you're so business-minded, you never get riled. What is it, honey?"

His concern was almost her undoing, but she kept her eyes glued to a picture on the far wall, trying to keep a tight rein on her hopelessly tangled emotions. They had never been tested so strenuously before.

"I'm not sure, Ben," she lied. "That man just rubs me the wrong way."

"That's an understatement," he grunted. "But there have been others over the years who have rubbed you wrong and you never got this upset. You've always kept your sense of humor before."

She rubbed her forehead in a weary gesture, closing her eyes only to see Steve's face dance before the screen of her mind. Quickly she opened them to banish the picture. "If you want to deal with him, it's all right with me. I just don't want anything to do with him."

"Perhaps if you got to know him better . . ." Ben's voice drifted away at the expression on her face.

"No. I don't think that will change things."

"And I can't see the advantages of sending a client of his potential away. How would I explain it? That my vice-president and right-hand woman has decided to act as an emotional female and turn her back on one of the largest accounts we've ever handled?" His logic was indisputable, and embedded small arrows of guilt in her skin. She had fought that image ever since she had left college. "Look, honey, this account could be your passport into this business." He spread his hands to encompass the building and everything within. "I'm thinking of retiring early," he hesitated. "And with the commission you could make on this job, you'd be able to buy out my share of the business with the rest in payments." He watched her carefully. She seemed to be struggling with something and he knew he had just thrown a monkey wrench into her plans. Anyone else would have grabbed at the opportunity. Normally she would have too.

Kathleen didn't really know what to say. Suddenly she was riding a razor's edge. She was damned if she did and damned if she didn't. After waiting for the chance to buy the business, could she really afford to turn her back on it now?

"Ben." She smiled to take the sting out of her next

words. "You're really a past master at dangling carrots, aren't you?"

Ben chuckled, realizing her decision even before she did. "Only in front of stubborn mules, honey."

She grinned then. Ben was a doll, and he was right. "It's a shame Ellen snapped you up, you know. You and I are so well suited."

He shook his head in mock regret. "Don't I know it, but I wasn't able to stay out of the marriage market long enough for you to be born and grow up!"

Ben suddenly sobered. "But it's your job to do the traveling, Kathleen. I'm too old for that stuff anymore, which is why I hired you in the first place."

"I know," she stated quietly.

"Good." Ben stood, suddenly reluctant to leave. "In that case I'll let you get back to work. Or would you like to call it a day and leave now?" He glanced at his watch. "It's already three o'clock and you could do with a little time off. I bet your mother hasn't seen you in ages."

"Her schedule is too hectic. I'm home when she's gone and vice versa."

"Well, go visit her now." He had gotten as far as the door when he remembered something else. Snapping his fingers, he stuck his head back in. "I almost forgot. That new number you just finished this morning looks so good I think it should stay in the line. What do you think?"

"Fine. Unless we get a customer who wants an exclusive on it. It would cost the earth, but I think it's lovely." She chuckled, proud of her accomplishment, and knowing Ben was stroking her.

61

"The only person with that kind of money just left the premises," Ben stated dryly before closing the door and shutting out her answer. Kathleen didn't have an answer anyway. He was right. Only Steve West could possibly pay for the exclusive rights to that material.

She reached for her purse. She wasn't going to give Stephen West another thought today. She deserved time off for good behavior and she wasn't going to let anyone ruin it.

The house was spotlessly clean and empty as usual. She walked up the stairs, her hand trailing the smooth bannister. Her bedroom door was open, the bed made, and everything dusted. Slipping off her shoes, Kathleen lay across the bed, her arms covering her eyes to keep out the bright afternoon sun. She was totally washed out. Steve West's devilish face danced in front of her, his mocking smile deriving satisfaction from her frustration. How would she be able to go through with his proposal without blowing her stack at him? Was there any way to not lose this order? She didn't know.

Kathleen sat up slowly as an idea formed. Just because she would be outfitting his newest playtoy didn't mean she would be in his presence. He wouldn't be there while she was working, would he? In all probability his short attention span would turn to more likely pursuits, directing him toward bright lights and willing women. His type of woman would be flashy, voluptuous, and ever-clinging to the Great Tin God. The helpless-female type who played to the macho stud. He was no different from most men, but he had the money to indulge himself.

Almost every man she had ever met had tried to plead his sorry case with her. He was lonely and looking for the perfect woman. And she was it. She was beautiful, charming, and so smart. Then they would insult her intelligence with their clumsy attempts at seduction. After living twenty-five years, she should have formed a tolerance level for it, but instead she just lost patience.

She stirred. Wasn't she supposed to have dreams and needs that needed fulfilling too? She knew there was no answer to her question, and that depressed her even more. She hadn't thought along those lines in a long time, and shouldn't have started now. After all, hadn't she finally made peace with herself? Wasn't she happy with her life just the way it was? Of course she was!

The telephone jangled into her thoughts and she reached toward the nightstand at the side of her bed.

"Kathleen? Glad I caught you." Ben's raspy voice crackled over the wire. "Steve West just called and asked us to attend a party at his hotel tonight. He thought we might want to meet the decorator of the polo club, plus a few other business associates who might be able to throw a little money our way.

"Go without me, Ben. I've already made plans for the evening." *Like filing my nails, washing my hair, staring at the ceiling.*

"No. If you don't go then we won't. Either we're a team or we don't do business at all," he stated matter-of-factly.

63

"But," she hesitated, remembering his earlier words. This account could mean the difference between her buying into the company now, or waiting several years. "All right, Ben, I'll meet you there."

"No. Ellen and I will pick you up at eight. Be ready," he growled, secretly pleased that she had capitulated. Perhaps if the two of them saw each other under less strained circumstances they might be able to dissolve their almost tangible differences. Ben had seen the glow in Steve's eyes and recognized it for what it was: admiration and desire to see Kathleen as a woman and not a business associate. And it might do her good to melt a little. She needed some fun and recreation. All work and no play . . .

By the time she was dressed for the party Kathleen had brought her sense of panic under control. No one was going to scare her away from her dream of owning this company. And that included Stephen West. She had worked too hard and long for this chance, and she knew she could do an excellent job with it. If he was willing to allow her the chance to show her stuff, then why should she balk? Old memories be damned. It was just a glimmer of recollection in the far past. That was all.

She glanced at herself in the mirror, pleased with her reflection. A sophisticated honey-haired woman in a deep chocolate-brown Grecian-style dress. It hugged her slim length of thigh and smooth hips without clinging too tightly to her small waist, flowing in a perfectly draped line. Her hair was loose, flowing over her shoulders in wisps and curls to frame her face perfectly. Small topaz and gold studs dressed her ears, with a matching ring complimenting her hand. Bronze sandals completed the picture. She was ready.

Her mother stood at the bottom of the stairs, her eyes showing her concern. She had never known Kathleen to be so cold and reserved as when she had discussed this cocktail party earlier.

"Are you sure you should go tonight? You look so tired, darling." She spoke softly, her hands fluttering in hesitancy. She was never calm in the face of her daughter's grim determination. Kathleen was as stubborn as her father had been, but with twice the business head, thank goodness. "There's something going on that you're not telling me."

"Relax, Mother. It's just a party for a client. It wouldn't be polite if I didn't go." She tried to calm her mother even though her own heart was thumping loudly in her ears.

"Yes, but . . ." A horn honked in the driveway and Kathleen reached for the delicate webbing of a pale ivory cashmere shawl.

"Don't worry. I won't be too late, but don't wait up for me." She kissed the air in her mother's direction.

They were in front of the plush hotel too quickly for Kathleen. She held on to Ben's arm tighter than she had ever thought possible. Thank goodness Ellen kept up a running conversation of triviality. She kept Ben's attention from focusing on herself.

They were whisked by private elevator up to the top floor, where it opened directly into a huge living

65

area. Glass windows on two sides gave a vista that couldn't be anything but real. One window faced downtown Denver, with the lights twinkling and cars moving, buildings of grace and smart clean lines displaying themselves. The other window displayed what Colorado was famous for . . . the distant outline of the Rocky Mountains. They were majestic and awe-inspiring, waiting patiently to enfold one in solitude, to heal with peace.

The room itself was filled with the Beautiful People. Kathleen recognized a few of the elite Denver society roster, while others held the indescribable stamp of wealth and power. Most of the faces were unknown to her, but she knew they were of the same retinue that seemed to follow the great host.

She glanced around, already wishing she had turned down this invitation. A black-coated waiter offered her champagne in a crystal glass and she took it. Looking up as she sipped, her eyes were caught by Steve's. He had obviously been watching her long before she had seen him. Slowly he smiled, then lifted his glass and gave a silent mock salute before sipping. It was a triumphant tribute to her attendance, but she knew he had never doubted her coming. He held all the aces and was confident of winning.

Determination came to the fore, wiping out all her plans of staying in the background. She, too, sipped her drink, raising an eyebrow in his direction before deliberately turning to give him her back, as if to say nothing mattered where he was concerned.

She scanned the crowd, searching and finding Ben and Ellen, who were still by the elevator talking to someone they obviously knew well. Ben glanced up and gave a wink and a grin before reentering the conversation he was having.

Kathleen still had her cashmere wrap slung over one shoulder and glanced around for a place to drop it. It gave her something to do by herself in a room full of strangers. From her outward coolness no one would have guessed that she was harboring a quivering mass of butterflies in the pit of her stomach.

"So you came after all, lady," Steve's voice murmured over her shoulder. She pivoted slowly, gathering all her forces before facing him. He was imposing, the smell of his aftershave tickling her nostrils, his look warming her skin.

"Don't call me that."

His gray eyes darkened as he smiled, gazing down at her. She knew he was remembering another time when she hadn't minded being called anything as long as she was in his arms, wrapped in his warmth, and her blush told him so.

"Why not? You remind me of one." His voice was pitched very low and he leaned forward in order to have only her hear his words.

"The standing-on-a-street-corner variety, I suppose?" she snapped, regretting it the moment she said it. Why was she carrying on a conversation with the one man she didn't want to have anything to do with?

"I was thinking of a prim, spinsterish type. Have you ever noticed how graceful they are? But if you touch them or praise them, they usually withdraw rather than allow their own sensuality to surface for all the world to see. They don't know what to do with compliments or soft-spoken words." He flicked her soft, webbed shawl. "Just like you."

For a moment all the sound was far away, and surrounding them was total silence. Kathleen forced her eyes away from his, glancing around the crowded room at anything and everything. She could hardly bear the attention he was foisting upon her, but her feet were firmly rooted to the spot.

But his hand once more demanded her attention as he brushed a lock of hair that sat on her soft shoulder, sending a chill down her spine.

"Keep your hands to yourself." Her eyes sparked brown fire, her breathing increasing to a faster pace.

"You look frightening when you're angry, but in reality you're harmless to those who want to take a chance and find out," he remarked calmly, a small smile curving his mouth.

"I wouldn't try out your theory if I were you." Her voice was hard and tight. Once again she was on the balcony with him, and once again he was touching her, making her shudder with anticipation.

"I won't rush you, Kathleen. You still scare too easily right now."

She couldn't keep the panic from showing as her face turned white and her hands clenched together. "Stay away from me, Steve West," she hissed, trying to keep her voice down as crowds milled around them, not wanting anyone to overhear her conversation but having difficulty keeping her temper. She ignored the fact that she felt frightened, more frightened than she had felt in the past four years.

"You've kept me away for the past four years, Kathleen. Don't think you can do that anymore." His voice was hard, his words short and terse, his silent message more frightening than his words. It sounded almost like a threat. "Or haven't you grown up by now?"

"I'm sure I wasn't the first to join you in fun and games and I realize I could never be the last as long as you're drawing breath, so go find a replacement for me. Find someone else's sandbox to build castles in. I don't want what you have to offer any more than you wanted what I had." Her bitterness came through, but instead of driving him away he gave a satisfied smile, much like a Cheshire cat. The palm of his rough hand trailed down her bare arm to send waves of warmth through her body. But she stood straight and tense, her eyes sparkling fire as a challenge. "Please. Go away and let me live my life without the excitement of your presence. I don't think I can stand too much more." She almost pleaded.

"And I thought you might have buried the memory," he murmured, ignoring her last words as if they had never been spoken. The texture of his voice stroked against her nerves like soft, worn velvet. His deep gray knowing eyes bore into hers, reading her soul and devouring it.

"And I'm surprised you didn't lose it among all the memories of those who followed in my footsteps," she snapped, resisting the temptation of looking into his dark sensuous eyes as they almost physically caressed her slim body.

A chuckle started deep in his throat to echo across

her skin. "Not remember the one who got away? Impossible!"

She could take no more. She stared at him, her anger clearly visible. "And that was all I was to you, wasn't I? The one who got away. Well, thank heavens I did, or I might have been dragged down in the mud you cover yourself with. Now, if you'll excuse me, I'll find my boss and tell him that I'm leaving. I didn't think I wanted to attend this party. Now I know I was right." She moved to leave, but he reached out and grabbed her arms in a viselike grip. She had finally roused his anger.

"Listen to me, my Kathleen, and listen well. I brought my business to your company because your reputation is good. I still want you to decorate those kitchens because your color sense is excellent. But from now on I'll stick on my side of the fence and you stay on yours." His eyes blazed down at her and she whitened from what his hand was doing to her, even in anger. He took a deep breath and continued, his voice less violent. "Now, if you can separate your business from personal life, then perhaps we can work together.

"You're the one who tried to mix the two!"

"It was a mistake," he stated unequivocally, lessening the grip on her arm. "From now on it will be business only. Agreed?"

Her throat choked at words too late to utter. He never knew the heartache she had gone through. And if she played her part right he would never know. She gave her head a sharp nod.

"Good. Now come over here and let me introduce

70

you to the decorator of the polo club. I think you'll like her."

Good as his word, he introduced her to an older woman, Anne Gonzales. She was as tall as Kathleen and slightly heavier, with a crown of lustrous blue-black hair that shone in the indirect lighting. She was charming, open, and very knowledgeable about her chosen work. She and Kathleen took to each other immediately, discussing problems of work conditions, colors, fabrics—everything that had to do with the industry.

"I don't understand why Mr. West wants a restaurant supply to do the kitchens. You could do it as well, I'm sure." They were relaxing on a toasty gold-colored wraparound couch that faced the mountains. Neither woman was vain enough to realize how well the surroundings acted as a foil for their individual beauty as they continued the discussion.

"I'm not so sure about that. I do know that the kitchen isn't my favorite place. Besides, Steve is right. It needs more appliances than I know about. The last time I cooked anything was fifteen years ago." She looked thoughtful. "I believe it was a baked potato and I burned it to a french fry."

They both burst into laughter, stopping only when Steve approached carrying two glasses of bubbling champagne, and handed one to each of them. His smile was warm and relaxed as he surveyed their apparent ease with each other. "I can see you two have a lot in common."

Kathleen could feel her nerves tightening and she rebelled once more. "Some people are much easier to

71

get along with than others," she retorted bitterly, much to Anne's surprise.

"And others become friends overnight then worry the fact to death," he stated tautly.

They were talking in cross-purposes and Anne felt an undercurrent she had not felt before, and was puzzled. "My good old-fashioned red, white, and blue heritage tells me that the conversation we're having is on my level. But my Mexican heritage, which is full of instincts and dire warnings, tells me something is being said that I don't understand at all." Her glance darted between Kathleen's closed face and Steve, sitting expressionless.

"Skip it, Anne," he stated curtly, rising to leave. "By the way, you might want to explain the setup of the polo club while you two are chatting. It would help Miss Bolton become acclimated more quickly." He was gone, leaving both women staring after him.

After an enigmatic glance at Kathleen, Anne changed the subject, explaining the layout of the cottages concisely, including a few of the color schemes of the more unusual ones.

". . . and that's all that's left now; the clubhouse kitchen and the cottages. I've completed the condominiums, but that wasn't any harder than doing an apartment house. Everything had to stay fairly neutral in color and design."

"Condominiums?" Kathleen questioned weakly, for the first time realizing just how large a project the polo center was.

Anne nodded her head. "There are other polo centers that are similar, such as the polo club in

Florida and there's another one in San Antonio, Texas. Steve visited them all and combined their best features, placing his own fortune on the line.

"Since his brother's accident Steve has taken over the family busines. Now everything is tied up in a corporation rather than owned singlehandedly. This polo idea was his from inception and I believe he wants to use it as a prototype for others."

"I didn't know his brother was in ill health," Kathleen murmured, once more confused about the image of the man she hated.

"Oh, he's not anymore, he just doesn't want the responsibility of the corporation back. He takes after his father, who spent more in one hour than most of us could spend in a year! But he never worked, except in spurts. Ted was the oldest and took over when his father died, but he never had the business sense that came so naturally to Steve. His only problem was he wanted Steve to work in the company but not make any decisions. Steve doesn't work that way, and went in the opposite direction, playing with the jet-setters in order to thumb his nose at the world." She had chosen her words carefully, realizing Kathleen knew nothing about Steve and his family, and realizing that somehow it was very important that she understood. Besides, it was no more information than could be gotten from a newspaper, if someone cared to look it up.

"I see," Kathleen muttered. Only she didn't. The man Anne spoke of so warmly had very little to do with the man Kathleen knew.

"Tell me more about the cottages. I'll need to

73

know more about the color schemes in order to judge what I'll need."

The evening went swiftly after that. Kathleen almost succeeded in dismissing Steve from her mind until she saw his lean, muscled frame out of the corner of her eye or heard the deep, rumble of his chuckle. At least with Anne to entertain her she was safe from his tricky tongue that spoke in riddles.

She left the party quietly, grabbing a taxi in the street after asking Ben to say the formal good-byes. She needed time to think and that could be done only in the privacy of her room. Everything was too confusing right now—she still wasn't sure what Steve's reasons for hiring her were. Was he telling the truth when he said that he had come to her company because of its reputation, or was there another reason, one that had to do with her? Her mind was too tired to reason it out.

Surprisingly enough, Kathleen went directly to sleep. Visions of Steve smiling down on her with a warmth shining from his gray eyes haunted her dreams. His expression turned stormy and she wanted to reach out and beg for his forgiveness, but she wasn't sure what she had done to make him angry. Then she felt her temper flare and he looked sad. The next morning she was still exhausted, as if she had run a marathon.

She ignored her mother's cold shoulder and intense looks over breakfast the next morning. She didn't need a censor in her life right now. Not when she couldn't make head or tail out of it herself.

By the time she walked into the office she was satisfied with her decision.

She stuck her head in Ben's office door. "Morning," she smiled. "I'm taking the West assignment."

Ben grinned through the stub of his cigar. "Good. He just called and I told him you would."

"What?"

He looked sheepish for just a moment before blustering, "Well, after last night and your cozy talk with Anne I just prejudged your answer. I didn't think you'd talk that long if you hadn't decided on accepting the job."

"You're impossible!" She grinned despite herself. Apparently she was easier to read than she thought.

"I know. That's what Ellen says," he chuckled, looking slightly guilty and loving it. "And they say females can't agree with one another!"

CHAPTER THREE

Christmas day weather was as pretty as a picture post card. The sunshine made the frosted branches of the trees glisten like sparkling diamonds and look as if they held hidden lights that twinkled a brilliance of their own. The sky was a cloudless blue with only small puffs of white hanging over the blue-gray silhouetted mountains. Kathleen idly watched from the living-room window as the clouds slowly moved across the sky. She played with a metallic piece of silver icicle trimming that had fallen off the Christmas tree, absently twirling it around her fingers.

"Kathy, would you plump up the couch cushions for me? Taylor should be here any moment, and I want everything to look just right," her mother fluttered at the doorway, her eyes scanning the already immaculate room for one out-of-place item. Everything was perfect. The house even smelled like

76

Christmas. The pine scent of the tree mingled with the aroma from various dishes in the kitchen—the turkey, stuffing, the sweetness of candied yams. Even the pungent odor of cranberry bread wafted through the air.

Kathleen did as she was told, smiling to herself for not resenting her mother's nervousness. Four or five years ago it would have upset her, but now she knew it was just a cover-up for a neat-freak.

"If I didn't know better, I'd say that Taylor Stitch was something unique, even without his crazy name!" she teased.

"I know." Her mother grinned. "His mother must have had an odd sense of humor to do that to a child. But I understand that until he was grown he was called Tad." She sniffed the already pungent air. "I think my fresh green beans are done." She hurried in the direction of the kitchen, once more engrossed with dinner preparations.

They had already opened the presents earlier that morning. Kathleen had given her mother a sterling silver comb and brush set. It was a replica of the one she had sold right after her husband had died. Along with it she gave her mother a new hostess gown and an intricately designed silver-white shawl. Kathleen had received a new dress, which she was now wearing. It wasn't really her style, but her mother had looked so happy when Kathleen had opened it that she didn't have the heart to tell her it was too revealing. It was soft jersey wool in a pale blue, with a deep V neck and small slit on either side that showed off more thigh than she cared to think about. It really was becoming, even if it was suggestive.

"I hear a car, dear. Would you check and see if it's Taylor?" her mother called from the kitchen. Once more Kathleen grinned. She'd never seen her mother so eager for company before. It was very touching and somehow sad.

She was standing at the open door as she watched the older man walk up the sidewalk, his steps dodging the icy spots the shovel had missed. He wore a heavily lined trench coat, but Kathleen could see a dark blue wool suit beneath it. A scarf was wrapped dashingly around his neck and a Homburg perched upon a too-large head completed his wardrobe. He even looked like a jolly old tailor.

"You must be Kathleen." He smiled jovially, both his gloved hands coming up to clasp hers, dancing them up and down in a strong grip. "I'm Taylor Stitch." He let go of her hands and put his in the air as if to shield himself. "And mind you, no jokes! I've heard them all."

The house became alive with the welcoming bustle of company. Taylor made the room dance with his deep voice, causing both Kathleen and her mother to chuckle delightedly on more than one occasion. They laughed at his jokes, listened to his more somber stories, and enjoyed his conversation. Kathleen even watched her mother blush at his compliments. He seemed to be just what the doctor ordered as far as her mother was concerned. And even Kathleen had to admit that it was nice to have a man's presence in the house again. It made the holiday more festive. After dinner they returned to the living room, all stuffed with turkey and mincemeat pie. Fresh coffee was the perfect touch to end the meal, as was the amaretto that accompanied it. Darkness decended and the glow from the fireplace filled the room with softened light, making this holiday cozier and more special.

When the doorbell rang, Kathleen, chuckling at one of Taylor's funny stories, went to answer it. It never dawned on her it could be anyone other than a neighbor calling to wish them a Merry Christmas. But as she opened the door a large shadow loomed in the darkness and she gasped softly as she reached for the overhead outdoor light, illuminating them both with the harsh yellow glare.

"You!" Her breath caught in her throat.

"It's cold outside. May I come in?" Steve questioned, his voice mocking her astonishment.

"Who is it, darling?" her mother called from the living-room entrance as she walked toward the still opened door, eyes darting inquisitively between the dark-haired stranger and her daughter's pale face. She came forward, her hand held out in greeting. "Hello. Please come in. I'm afraid my daughter thinks heating the outside is the thing to do, but I don't agree," she teased, pulling him in and shutting the door firmly behind her.

"Hello, Mrs. Bolton. I'm Steve West, a old friend and potential client of your daughter's." He gave her his best boyish grin, but Mrs. Bolton's warmth turned into an icy stare. Her hands froze in the act of helping him off with his coat. "Did I say something wrong?" He was surprised at how much the small birdlike woman suddenly resembled a mother bitch protecting her pups, growling a warning just before the bite.

"Mother, please." Kathleen found her voice, "Come in, Mr. West and make yourself at home." Of all the actions both Steve and her mother had expected from Kathleen, it had not been this. But instinct told her to treat the situation lightly.

Dark gray eyes studied her. "Thank you, I'd like that," he stated slowly as she took his arm and led him into the living room. Within minutes he was handed a glass of neat whisky and seated in a low comfortable chair, discussing the possibilities of more snow with Taylor.

"Excuse me," Kathleen murmured. "I'll get coffee and fruitcake." She made what she hoped was a graceful exit, taking a deep breath only when she reached the kitchen and could lean against the wall without having her trembling legs give from under her. Steve was here, but why had he come? Her mind searched for an answer but could find none.

The door opened and, as Kathleen expected, her mother came bustling in.

"What in heaven's name is going on and why is *that man* sitting in our living room looking for all the world like a guest when he should be tarred and feathered and sent on his way?"

Kathleen raised a hand, wearily pushing back the pale taffy-colored hair that clung to her neck in wisps. It was freezing outside and yet she was hot and damp with perspiration.

"Mother, Steve doesn't know anything about what happened after I left him four years ago, so why should we tell him? Just to make him feel sorry or to embarrass me? Either way, there's nothing to be done that can erase what happened."

"But to invite that man into the house as if he were a valued friend . . ." Her mother couldn't keep the intense stress from her voice. "Leaving a young girl to face the consequences of a pregnancy alone, not even caring . . ." Her voice broke on the remembered heartache.

Kathleen's voice was firm and detached. "As I see it, we have two choices. One, we can make the best of it, or two, we can embarrass everyone, including Taylor, and drag out the dirty laundry. Frankly I prefer not allowing Steve the satisfaction of knowing what a silly fool I was."

Her mother finally agreed rather reluctantly. The atmosphere was awkward when they returned to the living room, but in no time Taylor was back in the swing of the conversation and they all relaxed.

It was late when Taylor stood to leave. It had been such a nice day that even Kathleen was reluctant to see it end. Steve had also shown a side of himself she had never seen before. He could be charming and warm and witty, given the chance. A little whisper echoed in the back of her mind, *Isn't that how you first saw him? And didn't he still treat you like dirt? Stay away from him! Stay away!*

After his good-byes Kathleen's mother walked Taylor to the door and Kathleen and Steve were left in the room alone. Her heartbeat quickened to a faster tattoo, but pride would not allow her to let him see how much his presence affected her. Her eyes were cool, her expression calm but remote. Steve stood, his gray-eyed gaze never leaving her face as he walked directly in front of her, only stopping when he was almost touching. The crackling fire and Kathleen's heartbeat drumming in her ears were the only sounds in the room.

Steve's hand reached out, touching a lock of her hair, rubbing the softness between his fingers. "Thank you for this evening, Kathleen. It was nice," he stated simply, and she glowed before quickly shielding her feelings.

"You're welcome."

His eyes darkened and held a thoughtful, puzzled look. "Tell me something. Why was your mother so shocked at my name. Did she know about us four years ago? Is that it?"

"Yes."

"And, like you, she hates me." It was a statement, not a question. It didn't need an answer. "You're the injured party, and I'm the SOB that done you wrong. Is that how we're playing this?"

"I'm not playing a game, Steve." She tried to concentrate on the wall behind him. "So you'll have to play by yourself."

"And the game I'm playing is for high stakes, Kathleen. If you want my account, you'll have to play . . . if only to protect your own interests." He turned and walked toward the hall, leaving her feeling bereft and lonely.

"Steve?" She stopped him at the entrance. He

turned around slowly, facing her, giving her the full magnetism of his gaze. But the question was burning her tongue, the one she needed answered now. "Why did you come here tonight?"

"It was Christmas."

"But why here?" she persisted.

"I've spent enough Christmases in hotels. I wanted a change."

"Why not go to Ben or Anne or anyone else who was at your party the other night?"

Steve turned back toward the hall. He stood motionless for a moment and she waited, holding her breath, for his answer. She wasn't sure why it was so important, but it was. He shrugged his shoulders and moved toward the door.

"Good night, Kathleen."

"Good night," she finally whispered to the empty room.

The weeks that followed were busy ones for Kathleen. Once the holidays were out of the way business went on as usual. Clients hurriedly came and went. The showroom had to be revamped with every visit, catering to the needs of the individual customers. Ben finally took pity on Kathleen and hired an assistant. Her secretary took pity on her and filed more papers than nails. Things were looking up.

Kathleen ignored the rapid approach of February as if the month had grown horns and a tail. However, lurking in the back of her mind was her promise to visit the polo center by the first of that month, staying two weeks, and having the paperwork for the entire project finished by April first.

She had begun to choose designer-fabric swatches, color chips for pots, pans and other cooking utensils, pictures of other accoutrements such as various sizes of butcher block tables, wineracks, glassracks, utensil holders in wood and wrought iron. But somehow her heart wasn't ready to accept the fact that she was really going to Steve's polo ranch, and she procrastinated putting the entire package together.

Then there was the problem with her mother. At least once a week her mother would find an article on Steve in the gossip column of one newspaper or another. He had a riotous New Year's Eve party in New York. He was seen at the ballet with a young and beautiful starlet. He cut the opening ribbon of the new opera house in San Francisco. Then there would be mention of him in the weekly news magazines. Business in the West Hotel chain had risen fifteen percent in a time of recession. The West stock was one of the ten best picks of the year. And finally a polo center was rumored to be opening soon that would rival all the others in the United States. Kathleen's mother would wring her hands and continue to berate her daughter for even being civil to him. She pleaded and begged for Kathleen to stay home. She tried to talk Taylor into arguing with her, only it didn't work. He didn't know Kathleen and Steve's past history and couldn't understand her mother's aversion to Kathleen doing her job.

The last week in January found Kathleen even more harried than usual. She had put off all plans to attend the polo center, hoping for a miracle that hadn't come through. The next phone call destroyed her faith in miracles.

"Ms. Bolton, here," she muttered around a pencil clenched in her teeth. She was quickly running through the small samples of cloth hooked on a ring on her desk. They were all new and had just been delivered by the fabric factory.

"Hello, Ms. Bolton. How are you?" Steve's deep velvety voice mocked her formality, and the skin on her arms prickled. There was such an intimate depth of tone in his voice that it frightened her.

"Fine, Mr. West. Is there something I can help you with?" Was that her best crisp businesslike voice, or was that the sound of a bullfrog without a pond?

"I thought I'd give you the schedule of arrangements. I'll pick you up next Monday at eight o'clock sharp." His voice, too, sounded very businesslike. "And remember to pack jeans. The atmosphere there is very informal, especially now, with the workmen all over the place putting in the finishing touches."

"I'm afraid I'm just not ready, Mr. West." Kathleen didn't bother to figure out her reasoning, she just decided to act stubborn. He might as well learn now that she was not the type to drop everything and be ready whenever he clicked his fingers.

"That's funny. I just talked to your boss and he seemed to think you had everything under control. He even thought you could be ready before this weekend, but I told him it was impossible for me to leave that soon." His voice was filled with surprised innocence, but she realized he had blocked her effectively by discussing the trip with Ben first. "Of course, Miss Bolton, there are several things that come first on the list, only one of which is a beautiful woman," he stated smoothly, purposely reinforcing her belief in his life-style.

"Of course," she muttered bitterly, then, hearing just how churlish she sounded, began again, tempering her voice. "All right, Mr. West. I'll be ready. Only I believe I should drive my own car, just in case I need to return here for samples or something." She hoped it didn't sound like the lame excuse it was.

"If you need anything extra, I'll have one of the men pick it up. Some of the workers come into Denver on a daily basis." He was firm to the point of shortness. "So why don't you just stop running and do as your told, like a good little executive?"

Her embarrassment and anger were so acute she couldn't think of a retort. But it didn't matter because he had hung up the telephone. It took her all afternoon to simmer down, but when she did, she realized he was right. She had been visibly dragging her feet all the time, which gave away far more of her feelings than she wanted to. From now on she'd better watch what she said and did. All she had to do is be businesslike, thorough, and completely calm and rational. After all, it would only be a matter of two weeks. Fourteen days. For some reason, unknown to her, a small voice in the back of her mind laughed and laughed at her own naivete.

CHAPTER FOUR

Kathleen surveyed the three suitcases that sat in the entryway of her home. She hoped she had everything. Besides jeans and T-shirts, she had also packed two formals and a few business dresses. Hair dryer, makeup, and a small bag of accessories along with another bag of shoes to match her outfits were all in one suitcase. At least her packing was organized, even if her brain was going off in three different directions.

"I just don't see why you have to go. After all, the company really belongs to Ben Corrigan, not you, and it should be his responsibility to take care of the large customers." Her mother came close to whining and Kathleen gave an exasperated sigh. She didn't need any more excuses for canceling this trip. She had enough reasons of her own.

"I don't want to go into this again, Mother, if you

don't mind. Someday, if I'm a good little girl and say my prayers, plus work twice as hard as any man, I may own this company. I don't want to lose that chance." She gave her mother's slim, birdlike shoulders a hug to take away the sting of her words. "And you know that if I make any fuss over this that others may find out just why I don't want to work for Mr. West. We don't want that, do we."

"I know, dear. I just don't want to see you succumbing to that man's charms again. He wasn't worth it the first time and he certainly won't be worth it now! He reminds me of a practical-joke type of Christmas gift. He's all pretty paper and colored yarn, but there's no gift inside."

Kathleen was saved from responding by the doorbell. Steve was on time. The cold crisp air came in with him and the freshness that seemed to always come after a snowfall gave her the itch to be outside.

After greeting a decidedly cold mother, he turned to Kathleen, refusing to make any apologies or explanations to Mrs. Bolton for what he obviously thought was a personal matter. "You don't travel light, do you?" He eyed the luggage with a disarming grin.

"No, considering one of the suitcases holds samples and worksheets galore. Besides, I want to finish the job in a week if I can."

"No grass under your feet, is there?"

"And a rolling stone gathers no moss," she retorted. "You're not too original, Mr. West."

"No, but you seem to be." His voice dropped an octave as he leaned toward her, only to reach for one of the suitcases. Her heartbeat doubled at his nearness, then dropped back into its regular rhythm as he turned toward the door, his deep gray eyes recognizing in triumph the emotions that showed in her revealing expression.

She ignored him. Saying good-bye to her mother took only a minute. They had already said everything that needed to be said. She walked stiffly toward the car door, not bothering to help load the suitcases into the trunk. He was supposed to be the macho man, let him do his thing!

Kathleen hardly noticed the scenery as they left Denver behind and began the drive to Colorado Springs. The silence was stilted and Kathleen couldn't keep her mind on any one topic for long. All thought reverted back to the enigmatic man beside her.

Steve reached toward the dashboard to turn on the radio and select a station that played soft dreamy music. Kathleen had to smile. Her mother and Taylor Stitch called it elevator music and played it constantly. It was perfect for a soft background sound during conversation. A conversation she wasn't having at the moment . . .

"You know, this isn't your walk to the guillotine. You are allowed to enjoy yourself," he said dryly, a small grim smile tugging at his lips and indenting his cheeks enough to show deep dimples before they vanished in a mask of cynicism.

She was equally dry. "I'm glad, if only for my sake."

"Why the spitfire act? Four years ago you were all

cuddling and cooing like a kitten. Now you bear a closer resemblance to an alligator—all mouth."

"And if you know the animal world at all, then you'll remember which of the two is the more dangerous, and stay away." She tried to control the trembling in her voice, but it was impossible. His words hurt, though they carried just enough of the truth for Kathleen to be ashamed. Several minutes later she had made a decision. They had a week or two to work together. She might as well offer the olive branch now and try for some semblance of harmony.

"What in hell is the matter with you, Kathleen? We met four years ago, had a short fling, and now I'm some type of monster! I don't get it! What in heaven's name could have happened to you between then and now to make you turn on me like this? Or do you react this way with every male?" His eyes narrowed as he glanced over at her tightly clasped hands.

"Look, Mr. West. You and I just aren't meant to get along, yet here we are, doing business with each other. If I promise to stick to my business of doing the best job I possibly can, then certainly you can keep from needling me. Perhaps we can both get through the next two weeks without a flare-up, and everyone can be happy." She turned in her seat, watching him closely. "What do you think?"

"I think you're wrong." His glance locked with hers for a second, and his eyes told her all she didn't want to know. She could see his appreciation of her attributes, but his scorn was there also, and she wasn't sure why she deserved that. "When we're together we become a volatile mixture. It's not a matter of oil and water; it's gasoline and matches." His mouth tightened ominously. "But I'm willing to keep my distance as long as you do the same. I'll never come any closer than you allow, Kathleen, so you'd better keep a watch on your own actions. Understood?"

"I've never done anything to provoke you!" she sputtered angrily.

"Just like a woman to deny her own provocative actions. Don't forget, I didn't force you to do anything, then *or* now. It takes two."

Her head bent forward to hide the rising blush of her cheeks. "Please, Steve, I don't want to relive all that again." Her voice held so much sadness and he was suddenly frustrated that he couldn't hold her in his arms. Instead he cursed under his breath in frustration, ending all conversation for both of them for the rest of the trip.

An hour of silence later Steve turned off the main road and onto a dirt path that was obviously being worked on by the highway department. The car weaved and bucked in slow motion as they passed several steel gates, all opened by a small metal box he kept in a holder under the dashboard. The flat and treeless grazing land was surrounded by the tall, craggy Rocky Mountains. Just ahead Kathleen could see a large copse of aspen. Through some of the sparser areas she glimpsed small cottages, a larger structure, and one or two barns. Suddenly new pavement led, like the yellow brick road, right into a land of Oz. The lodge was one of the most beautifully architectured designs Kathleen had ever seen. Directly in front of the winding drive was a three-storied lodge in nature-tinted gray timber and sun-shaded smoked glass windows that rose from top to bottom of the impressive building like tall sentries. She couldn't tell if there was more glass than wood or if it was the other way around. Steep, sloping roof lines, engineered in various angles, wouldn't allow the snow to collect. A low wooden sign on a post proclaimed the name WILD WEST POLO & SHOW CLUB and in front of what looked to be a restaurant was a sign reading CHUKKER CLUB.

"It fits," she murmured dryly, flicking her eyes from the sign to Steve, and his eyes crinkled, his mouth forming a half smile.

"The *W* in *wild* was actually supposed to be an *M* but the sign company made an error."

"I'll bet."

He chuckled. "You're right. It's supposed to be just what it is. But I should have known you'd prefer a mild man, someone you could browbeat into your mold."

"A mild man is sensitive, not browbeaten," she stated, wishing she hadn't said the words as soon as she spoke them. She sounded like an old prude.

"A mild man goes to great extremes not to argue, which means you'd win on all points. You wouldn't be happy with that type of man for long, my Kathleen."

"And why not?" She tried to ignore the warmth the possessive sound his voice evoked.

"You're a very independent lady and you need someone who understands that and allows you just so much rope before hauling you back into line. You couldn't respect someone you could trample all over. You need a mate with the same characteristics you have so you can deal with him on your level of intelligence, your level of intensity and passion."

"My God, you really think you know what you're talking about, don't you?" She was incredulous. His affrontery knew no bounds! She ignored the small thread of truth that wove through the fabric of his words. It was too upsetting to see anything other than what she wanted to see. "Did it ever dawn on you that you aren't really a psychologist and can't help others with your pearls of wisdom? That in fact you may be totally wrong?"

Steve pulled up under the canopy-covered entrance of the club, its newness showing the distinct color coordinating process: grey, green, and rust. Very striking and exceptionally subtle.

Turning in his seat, Steve gave Kathleen a stare that ate into her private interior where all her innermost secrets were kept. She involuntarily pulled away, leaning against the outer door. Suddenly his look left her breathless.

"No," he answered matter-of-factly, and stepped out of the car, leaving her anger boiling impotently. The large double doors were carved and weathered cypress, a beautifully intricate design set off by the simplicity of the building itself. Steve ushered her in, the heat from his hand on her arm burning through her coat to her skin. She walked stiffly, her head high and her heart fluttering against her breast. She followed him through the large, circular lobby and over to the right side where a dimly lit restaurant overlooked a serenely landscaped ice pond. Benches surrounded the edge along with dwarf evergreens and small flowerbeds, now empty. A dimly lit ice pond could be seen just outside the windows of the restaurant on the right side of the large lobby.

On the far end of the lobby was a room she assumed to be the bar. His mocking gaze told her he had once again read her mind as he almost pushed her ahead of him into it, then walked silently toward the wall holding a large ornate cabinet.

"We keep the guest-cottage keys here until the buildings are opened to the public. That way we know exactly who is in which cabin and what they're supposed to be doing in there."

"Important to know, I'm sure."

"Not only important, but necessary."

He dangled a key from his fingers. "This will be your cabin. It's closest to the office. You will have all your meals in the restaurant, but other than that, you can use the cabin as your office."

Kathleen cleared her throat. "I thought the restaurant wasn't opened yet. I thought the complex wasn't complete."

"Most of the workers stay here while we're under construction. We have to feed them, and that's the simplest way." He raised a darkly etched eyebrow. "Any other questions?"

"None, thank you." She snapped the keys away from him, anger rising once more to return in full.

94

She turned to make her grand exit, but his next words stopped her.

"Don't you want to know where your cottage is, Miss Bolton?" His husky voice ran in a primitive dance pattern along her already taut nerves.

He took a step closer and suddenly she felt both free and claustrophobic at the same time. The old push-pull emotions that he always aroused when he was near were present again, and just as uncontrollable.

"Stay away from me." Her voice shook as he ate up the small space between them. "I don't need your form of punishment, Steve. Just stay away."

He quirked one brow, arrogant and assured. "Are you that frightened of your own reaction to me, my Kathleen?" His warm breath fanned her lashes and she glanced down, only to see the mat of chest hair peeping from the open collar of his tan silk shirt. Her hands itched to feel his exposed skin against her palm, to play against the masculine, toned muscles. . . . Her eyes darted back to his face.

"Of course not." She wet dry lips with the small tip of her tongue then stroked the bottom of her teeth provocativly. Her heart was beating like a trip hammer against malleable metal and it showed in the small nerve at the base of her throat.

"Oh, Kathleen," he sighed, his hands intimately spanning her small waist. "Why do you always have to be so prickly? Who could have hurt you so to make you back away from every man you meet?"

Her voice was husky with somersaulting emotions only his hands could evoke and she answered without thinking. "A rat who turned his back on me when I needed him most. I was just another toss in the hay to you, wasn't I?" Her eyes searched for a denial, but instead she saw the gleam of triumph. Once again she had fallen into his neatly set trap and allowed her feelings to show.

Anger flooded her at his reaction and, without thinking, her hand swung up to sting across his face, her small ring twisting to make a narrow gash along his jawline. His grip tightened until she thought he would break her in two and she struggled to break loose, a feeling of panic invading her senses. Then suddenly she was standing deserted and alone in the center of the room.

Steve turned his stiff back on her and walked to the large wooden desk. The intercom was pushed and he barked an order into it. By the time he hung up, a young, dark-haired girl with a winning smile was standing in the doorway. She glanced at Steve, then to Kathleen.

"Hi," the secretary grinned. "I'm Merrie and I think I'm supposed to show you to your cottage." She winked, impish and friendly, and Kathleen took to her right away.

"Is there someone to carry my luggage?" She hoped her voice wasn't quivering as badly as her knees were knocking.

"I'll have someone bring it along shortly." Merrie led the way out of the room and through the lobby toward the front door Kathleen had entered earlier.

Her eyes stung as she realized that all day Steve had tried to be warm and friendly toward her and she

96

had shunned him. And now, when she wanted his warmth, she had not been able to show it. She was a fool! He had brought her here to work, not to be his playmate! She had a job to do and he had hired her to do it, and that was all.

Merrie led her toward the back of the club and to the other side of the pond. The path was stone, bordered by a small hedge as it wound through the tall forest-green pines and silvery aspens.

The cottage, if one could really call a place as large as a home that, was also of redwood. It mimicked the style of the clubhouse and fit snugly in the small clearing.

"This is furnished with everything you'll need for right now." Merrie opened the door with the key dangling from her waist, ignoring Kathleen's duplicate in her hand. "You can see the other cottage over there." She pointed toward the right side of the cabin. "They're all spaced about this far apart and go completely around the ten polo fields."

The room they entered was spacious. A large picture window overlooked a deck, which in turn overlooked the primitive mat of natural forest. Vines entwined and climbed the trees to exit around the small clearing. More miniature evergreen sat on the deck in large clay pots, some gaily decorated, some a natural reddish-gray.

It took Kathleen a while to focus on the living room itself . . . and it was beautiful. The natural stone wall they encountered when they walked in formed the entryway, but as Kathleen walked around it she saw it was a fireplace with a fire merrily blazing away. The couch was circular, what designers usually called a pit couch or playpen. It was dark russet with tan and rust throw pillows for accent. In one corner was a large, obviously old and expensive bentwood rocker. This was no cheap imitation. On the seat was a needlepoint cushion of a castle with a knight in armor carrying a damsel in distress on his steed.

To one side of the cottage was a small but complete kitchen done in bright lemon yellow and brilliant white. The opposite wall led to the bedroom and an enormous bath.

"All the comforts of home . . . and then some," Kathleen muttered, wondering how many people had the money to afford such accommodations. This was indeed luxury.

"That's our boss. Steve West goes first class or not at all," Merrie stated dryly, and Kathleen realized she was not only loyal but proud of her boss's accomplishments. It showed in her face and hazel eyes.

"Have you known him long?" Kathleen hoped her voice sounded casual.

"About ten years," Merrie admitted reluctantly. "Three years ago I went to work for him in the Florida office. When this place opened up he called and asked me to be his secretary. I jumped at it. I love working here."

"You must enjoy it."

"Andy and I both do." Merrie smiled her explanation. "Andy is my son. He's almost four years old now and has never been happier than since we've been here. When we lived in the city I had to leave him in a nursery school all day and we didn't get to see much of each other. Now I get to see him all the time."

"And where is he now?" Kathleen walked slowly toward the glassed wall and stared out at the woods beyond. It was a peaceful scene, the woods trimmed in ice and snow, the pristine whiteness of it all bringing light into the room.

"He's in the kitchen with the cook, Mrs. Andrews. She's a doll. You'll love her." Merrie checked the kitchen cupboard then turned with a grin. "If you need anything other than coffee, come into the restaurant. Dinner is between five and eight o'clock." Within a minute they had said good-bye and Merrie was gone. Kathleen could hear her muffled steps on the front walk, then nothing.

She crossed her arms and stared unseeingly at the winter scene outside. *Dear God, let me get through these next two weeks. Let Steve find other things to do beside haunt my waking and sleeping hours. Let me complete the job quickly and be able to leave his influence as quickly as possible.*

But he still evoked up her long-buried emotions. His virile magnetism wrapped Kathleen in a blind cocoon until all she could see and feel was his presence. She knew it and it frightened her. And he knew it too.

She hugged her arms closer to ward off the chill. "Nonsense!" she stated emphatically to the ghosts of her mind. "Nonsense!"

What her tired brain needed was a nap, she told herself as she curled up in the soft curve of the couch.

Her dreams were of soft clouds and bright spring days. Trees dipped in early morning dew, sparkling with a thousand tiny lights. A brook gurgled merrily, the banks soft with the brilliant green of thick plush moss. The setting was perfect. When the prince chuckled and softly kissed the side of her neck, Kathleen smiled, in love with life, the setting, with him. His lips teased hers, slowly, taunting her with the promise of more, and she reached up to draw him closer. Her heart sang with a happy song she didn't know the words to, but the melody beat in rhythm to her pulsing heart. Her limbs turned molten under his gentle caressing, aching to be held to his muscled body. He must have understood her need, for his hands clasped her tighter to him. She wiggled into the soft haven of his arms, wonder and delight filling the corners of her mind. One hand curved and cupped her breast as if weighing a great treasure and her heart skipped a beat before a sigh escaped her parted lips. Her eyes opened slowly and she stared into his. They were a soft gray, filled with tenderness and mirth.

His lips came down and captured hers, teasing them open by his very passivity. Her arms curved around his neck and she smiled slowly, reveling in the feeling of total peace and contentment.

"Mmm," she murmured seductively.

"You like?" His voice was low, his breath light on her lips.

"I like." She curved her fingers into the thick vitality of his hair, feeling the springy healthiness of it.

"I would have come sooner if I had known of your

100

reception," Steve murmured huskily, then bent over to take her lips with his again, touching her soul once more, firing her with ecstasy.

"What are you doing here?" Her dream was complete now. He was here.

"I brought your luggage and found Sleeping Beauty. Being the prince of a fellow I am, I had to kiss you awake." He soothed her hair back from her furrowed brow, a small smile teasing the corners of his mouth as he watched her mind slowly work out the puzzle.

"My suitcases?" she asked when she suddenly realized where she was. This wasn't four years ago. This was now!

Steve watched the change of her expression and his grin grew deeper, his hands tightening on her waist. "Oh, no, you don't. Don't disappear on me now, my love. I just found you again after all this time. You won't escape so readily this time." Kathleen struggled against him, her eyes darkening to golden brown flames of fire.

"Let me go! Now! You had no right to kiss me!" Her voice, filled with contempt, lowered to a growl.

He flinched visibly, then his expression hardened, the muscle at the side of his jaw clenching and fixing her eyes on the small scab where her ring had dug into his flesh. He had deserved it, she tried to tell herself, ignoring the small twinge of guilt that tugged at her.

"And I thought you had changed your mind." His voice was mocking.

Her eyes opened wide, incredulous. "Did you honestly believe I'd be willing to pick up where we left off four years ago?" She laughed, a harsh sound that resembled a sob. "Four years may be a long time for you, but for me it isn't long enough."

He released her shoulders as if she were a red hot poker, and stood, towering over her prone form on the couch. She was wrinkled and sleepy and her blouse was loosened from her skirt. Suddenly she felt small and vulnerable and stood quickly, eyeing him across the expanse of the couch.

"Did I say something you didn't already know, Mr. West?" She taunted him softly, unable to resist one more jab. He raked her over from head to foot, then looked into her eyes as if he saw nothing at all. It was a cold, empty stare, and one that chilled her to the bone.

"I hoped that that cold exterior you project was a facade. But I was right. You're cold and devoid of any emotion, let alone honest ones. My error." He turned to leave. "Believe me, it certainly won't happen again."

Then he was gone.

Kathleen sank back on the cushions, her head in her hands. The pain of desolation was strong, but so was her determination. After five minutes of feeling sorry for something she couldn't recognize, she stood and straightened her clothing, willing herself to go through the motions of unpacking and rearranging. It was time for her to slip into her business-as-usual routine.

CHAPTER FIVE

She ate with Merrie and her son, Andy, that night at a table overlooking the pond that separated her cottage from the club. The food was excellent, the coffee fresh, and the atmosphere was subdued.

Andy was a doll of a little boy. His dark head was constantly in motion, reminding Kathleen of brown seaweed on the ocean bottom. He had at least three cowlicks and they all turned every which way, making him look more impish than even his pixieish face decreed.

"An' now, Mommy, can I have the ice cream, huh?" he interrupted for the fifth time during their conversation. His hand pulled on his mother's arm to insure her attention. "Please? I ate ever'thing."

"I see, Andy." Merrie's tone was laced with exasperation, but Kathleen could tell she wasn't really angry with the child, especially when she gave him such a delicious hug. "Ask Tim if he would be kind enough to serve you some. And remember your manners!" Tim was one of the younger college students who worked part time as a busboy.

They watched him skip to the tall, slender, and slightly awkward boy, almost demanding his ice cream right now. The only difference between this demand and others would be his winning smile.

"I know I spoil him terribly, but he's leaving tomorrow to visit his grandmother and I won't see him for a whole month," Merrie stated wryly, excusing her permissive behavior. And Kathleen chuckled. Merrie might have looked guilty, but she certainly wasn't repentant!

Kathleen was chuckling when she glanced up to find that Steve West had just walked in the door, a beautiful blonde at his side. She was draped on his arm as if she were a clinging crepe dress and he was a hanger, Kathleen thought cattily before squelching down the stab of pain that pierced her breast.

"Oh, no. Talk of the devil," Merrie murmured, picking up her cup with both hands to shield her face.

"Who is she?" Kathleen deliberately played with her napkin, keeping her eyes focused downward.

"That's the devil herself, Deborah Powers. She has a place in Aspen but comes over just enough to cause a commotion with the men and Steve in particular. I can't stand her."

"Because she's so beautiful?"

"Because she ignores me," Merrie retorted dryly,

looking up just in time to watch the beautiful couple weave through the tables toward them.

They reached the table and Merrie gave a glance toward Kathleen, who was looking down at her napkin, and Deborah, who was looking out the window, a bored expression on her face.

"You remember Deborah Powers, don't you, Merrie?" Steve questioned silkily before turning to Kathleen. But she was ready for him with an innocent stare as blank as his had been earlier. "Kathleen Bolton, this is Deborah Powers, a close friend and my . . . guest for the evening."

"How do you do, Miss Powers." Kathleen was calm and quiet. Not even the other woman's scrutiny was able to pass her barrier. Bright blue eyes stared down at her. "Are you one of the employees, too, Miss Bolton? I don't remember seeing you here before."

"I'm here to coordinate the appliances for the cottage kitchens."

"I see." The blonde narrowed her eyes at the beauty in front of her, then pulled on Steve's arm. "I'm hungry, darling. Can't we go to your place and have something sent in?"

He ignored her. "Did you enjoy your meal, Miss Bolton? Was it up to standard?" His voice held a note of a sneer that made his date's eyes light up with interest.

"Very much, thank you. I even enjoyed the company." She stood slowly, her eyes level with the other woman's. "But now I think I'll enjoy the solitude of a walk back to my cottage." Kathleen hesitated momentarily, smiling sweetly at Merrie, then nodding her head at the couple in front of her. "Good night all."

Her head was high as she made her way out of the dining room. She picked up her coat from the chair at the main desk and continued walking out the building and along the path toward the bridge and to her cottage. For reasons that were best left unexplored, Kathleen ached with the thought of Steve and Deborah together, later, in the dark of his apartment, with soft music and brandy . . . No! Forget it! She would keep her calm if it was the last thing she did!

Kathleen kept her mind and hands busy, putting wood on the fire, making notes on catalogs she would need in the morning. She kept totally engrossed in her work, absently sipping on a cup of instant coffee she had made for herself. Her thoughts slowly left the scene in the dining room and entered the world she knew best—business. Her mind whirled with ideas, thoughts that needed jotting down, premises that could be buoyed up with complementary color schemes. If she wasn't jotting notes, the pencil was in her mouth, her teeth bruising the soft wood. When she heard a doorbell peal she glanced up in surprise. She had no idea the house even had one!

"Miss Bolton?" Tim stood on the porch. "The boss told me to send this over for you. He thought you might want it for the morning." A large laminated paisley tray held milk, sugar, instant chocolate, half an apple pie still in its tin pan, and English muffins along with a few eggs.

flannel shirt, a heavy sheepskin jacket, and a cowboy hat.

"Since you don't have your phone yet I thought I'd let you know I ordered a desk for you." He glanced over his shoulder as muffled conversation drifted closer to them. Two men laden with cleaning equipment were coming toward her cabin. Suddenly the newly installed phone rang, and Steve's face took on a sheepish look. "It looks like Merrie told you already."

Kathleen couldn't help but chuckle, for right behind the cleaning crew came two more men struggling with a large metal desk. "Merrie didn't tell me half as much as she should have."

"Obviously not," he chuckled companionably as he stepped back to allow the men entrance. "I'll give Merrie a call and ask if there are any more surprises in store for you. Then you can write me a small grocery list, so when I run into town later I'll be able to pick supplies up for you."

"Merrie's here now." Kathleen stalled for time, reluctant to have him come any closer to her as he made a move to step in.

The phone rang again and Merrie yelled, "Eureka!"

"In that case"—Steve eased himself into the doorway—"let me make sure they get this thing in without banging the door down. Why don't you write that list, hmm?"

The list was made quickly and Kathleen handed it to him along with a twenty-dollar bill. Steve's brows raised at the sight of the money. "Planning ahead for a siege?"

"No, just privacy." Clear brown eyes stared defiantly at smoky gray ones. The men grunted as they placed the desk in front of the window. The telephone man began putting his tools away. Merrie stood at the entrance of the kitchen, watching everything.

But neither Steve nor Kathleen noticed anyone. They could have been alone and carrying on a long and intimate conversation for all they were aware of the commotion surrounding them. Old scenes replayed in their heads. Scenes of the night they first met and laughed at old jokes, danced to old tunes, stared into each other's eyes and silently declared that this was a magical night . . . When the door slammed for the first time the spell was broken.

Kathleen glanced around, embarrassed and hoping no one noticed them staring like two teenagers in the throes of first . . . not love, but heat. She had never loved and would not start now!

It was late afternoon before the workmen, Merrie, and the cleaning crew were out of her small chaotic haven. Others had delivered stationery, folders, pens, and pencils. She now had a full-fledged office.

She quickly made notes to herself of other items she would need. A map of the grounds and the locations of the other cabins would be helpful, along with the master key to the cottages.

When Steve knocked on the door later Kathleen knew instinctively who it was. Her skin prickled at the first sound. He couldn't reach the doorbell on the

110

side since his hands were full of grocery bags. He grunted as she reached for one, surprised at how heavy they were. She peeped into the top of one bag, but it was too difficult to see through a loaf of bread and a box of crackers.

He followed her into the kitchen, the scent of the crisp clean outdoors reaching her nostrils and telling her just how close behind her he was, and she hurried to stretch the space. But when she turned to place the bag on the countertop, he was directly behind her. He not only smelled of the outdoors, but of good leather and a tangy trace of aftershave. Her stomach knotted as she realized just how small the efficiency kitchen was.

"If you were bread and I were butter, we'd be ready for breakfast." He grinned, the smile working up to his smoky gray eyes. A dimple showed in his chin and the atmosphere relaxed considerably. He wasn't teasing or taunting her, just enjoying light conversation.

"I think the kitchens were made small to eliminate men helping during their vacations," she retorted, pulling a few of the foodstuffs from the bag and maneuvering around until she could open the refrigerator door. "Why don't you sit at the bar and I'll put on a pot of coffee." Her statement startled both of them. She certainly hadn't meant to invite him to stay. It had just popped out!

"Accepted." His serious expression belied the twinkle in his eyes, and caused a quickening of her heartbeat. He knew the invitation was accidental, but he wasn't gentleman enough to gracefully withdraw.

She glanced at him surreptitiously through her lashes. His bored expression, the one he used to wear four years ago, was gone. A lively curiosity lit his eyes now. She was a bug under a microscope and he was enjoying the fun of watching to see if she would squirm.

"Four bottles of wine?" She held up one dark bottle, knowing automatically that the vintage was more than she could afford.

"Compliments of the house." Steve reached into the inside pocket of his coat, pulling out a long thin cheroot. He raised it in question and she ignored it, still intent on the wine bottles in front of her.

"I forgot the brand you requested and retrieved a few bottles from our own wine cellar. Perhaps you can cultivate your palate while you're here. It was available and didn't cost me a cent more than wholesale, which brings it down to your cost."

She couldn't think of a reason not to accept it, yet her pride made her hesitate.

"If you place it in the refrigerator, I'm sure you'll find a use for it." His mouth turned grim, his sudden irritation showing through what had been a calm exterior. "And if you don't use it by the time you leave, then we'll place it back in the cellar with the rest of the stock."

Without another word she took the bottles and lined them up on the top shelf of the refrigerator.

Steve took a deep drag of his cheroot, his eyes narrowing on the slight bounce of her breasts as she placed the groceries where they belonged. "They

112

need to be kept at an even temperature to retain their best flavor.''

"I'll drink them fast." She continued to empty the bags, trying not to notice his stare even though her body seemed to move more sensuously knowing he was watching. She wished the water would boil. The sooner she served him his coffee and got rid of him, the better off she'd be.

"Why are you so contrary and cold?" His voice was low, but Kathleen heard every nuance of it. It purred with warmth and a touch of perplexity.

She smiled with a saccharine sweetness. She tried hard to remember why he was her enemy, but her mind wasn't really functioning rationally. She forced herself to answer. "I have to be when there are so many bullies around to take advantage."

"Oh, I see. You can't take criticism." His gaze was still hidden by smoke, but she knew there was a mocking light in his eyes.

Kathleen stopped playing with the brown paper bags and faced him, hands on hips. Her brown eyes turned a sherry color as her anger mounted. "Tell me, Steve. Why, after all these years, would you hire me just to ride me like this?" A blush tinged her cheeks when she recognized her bad choice of words.

"Riding you *like this* wasn't what I had in mind at all." He grinned, obviously enjoying her blush. "But I'm sorry. You're right, I have been making things difficult and I promise to stop it right now if you promise to thaw just a little bit and not freeze me with your eyes." He looked like a young boy scout with his hand in the air and his deep dimples showing. Kathleen didn't know whether to be angry or laugh. She laughed.

"Truce?" She held out her hand and he leaned forward to clasp it in his work-roughened one, almost caressing it, sending shivers up her arm she was hard pressed not to show.

"Truce," he stated solemnly.

They grinned at each other like a couple of children before the water bubbling on the stove caught Kathleen's attention. She turned quickly to tend to it and away from the almost intimate touch of the enigmatic man across the counter from her. As long as he stayed there she was safe. She just wasn't sure what she was safe from; her own whirling emotions, or his ever-pressing presence.

She served him coffee, black, then made her own with a dab of cream, hoping he didn't notice her shaking hands. She could still feel the pressure of his hand over hers when they shook, and rubbed her palm along the side of her thigh in order to rid herself of the tingling sensation.

By mutual consent they left the kitchen and wandered into the living room. They sat on the couch and stared into the fire, the companionlike atmosphere lulling her into a false sense of security. She felt safe, and warm, and comfortable. And even Steve seemed to enjoy the mood. She was both relieved and sorry when he broke the silence.

"How long have you been with Corrigan's?" His voice was soft, almost a musing tone, and she easily followed his lead.

114

"Four years." She sipped her coffee, her eyes still watching the dancing flames.

"And you've already become vice-president." It was a statement not a question.

"You make it sound as if I just walked into that position." She grinned, glancing at him, surprising herself that there was no feeling of animosity. "I worked almost every night and weekend to achieve that post."

"Do you like it?"

"Yes." There was a wealth of meaning in that single word. How else could she tell him of the thoughts that drove her crazy when she was by herself, alone at night, unless she was so tired that she could drop. Work was the panacea that kept her private thoughts at bay.

"You enjoyed it so much you never found time to marry?" He probed deeper, and this time she looked him square in the eye.

"Yes."

Suddenly his gaze iced over and a sneer tugged at his mouth, making him seem cold and hard. "But I'll bet you didn't need to do that, did you? There were always men about who could give you what you needed without your commitment to them."

She was the accused. Her heart beat faster than before, but she kept her gaze level. She would never let him know how much his words hurt.

"Once I was set on the path to 'ruin' it was an easy road to follow. Especially with such a tender and loving teacher." The flame that lit his dark gray eyes blazed to almost consume her, but she didn't back away from his anger. Instead she felt herself growing taller and more dignified. She had paid him back in coin for just a few of his hateful remarks.

"For someone as coldhearted as you are, I would imagine it would be a snap," he taunted softly, making her breath hiss in her throat.

"It makes it easy on you to believe that, doesn't it? It never dawned on you that you've always been able to do the same thing? Or is it the old double standard. You can get what you need without commitment, but no woman can do the same?" The lump in her throat was an open sore, and she swallowed to release her voice. But it didn't work.

"Some women think love and commitment go hand-in-hand."

"What do you want from me, Steve?" She knew. He wanted her pride in the dust. He wanted to laugh and sneer at her, to hurt her. She just didn't know why.

"I'll be repentant as you want me to be. I'll even apologize for the mess I made in your life . . . if I did make a mess. But so far all I've seen is a cold, heartless woman who couldn't warm up in a man's arms if her life depended on it. Prove to me I'm wrong about you, Kathleen. Prove it." He sat back, resting against the soft cushions of the couch and watched the myriad expressions flitting across her face, his own hiding whatever thoughts lay hidden behind his smoky eyes.

In future hours Kathleen would think of his words and her actions, and would never understand what had gotten into her to make her act the way she did.

116

She placed her coffee cup on the table and turned toward him. As if in slow motion her hands raised to cup each side of his face, stroking the firm line of his jaw, her thumb finding the small burrow that made the dent in his chin. Her golden-brown eyes opened wide to stare into his to see the flame of his desires there before she let her lashes fall to take in the firm, chiseled outline of his mouth. She placed her lips over his in a gentle but insistent kiss. He was passive to her touch, not moving, but allowing her any liberties she cared to pursue. When her tongue stroked around his closed mouth he opened and allowed her entry as they exchanged warm breath for breath. Tongues matched taste for taste, each feeling the heat and movement of the other. Her heart accelerated its pounding in her ears, drowning out any noise, including his own shortened gasps. Her tongue touched his teeth before seeking the inner soft tissue of his mouth until she felt him respond to her kiss. Her hands learned the outline of his neck, the slope of his shoulders, his biceps, then back again. Still his arms lay placed by his side. She wiggled closer, hoping to receive a reaction, any reaction, to show that she was getting to him. One hand stole down to slowly unbutton his shirt, her nails teasing the furry flesh beneath the silk. She ran her palm across his chest, stopping only when she reached the perimeters of his nipples, taut and standing, just as hers were beneath her sweater. Her lips moved, sucking gently on his bottom lip, then she teased him into thinking she was trying to devour him once more. She retreat-

117

ed, then attacked, then retreated again, trying to pull a reaction from him. But there was none.

With tears stinging just behind her eyelids she pulled away. Only then did he react. With a groan his arms came up and wrapped around her to press her to him, his stroking hands sliding down her back only to reach up under Kathleen's sweater and quickly undo the snap of her bra, releasing her from its bondage and allowing his hand easy access to her satiny fullness. He cupped one breast, expertly teasing her taut nipple until she thought she would cry out in delight. Her head swirled with desire, a multitude of colors ran rampant behind her lids as a deep-seated want grew to an ache in the pit of her stomach. A moan escaped her throat and Steve answered with a taunting pressure of his mouth, silently chasing the warmth of her tongue back into her own sphere and ravishing her on her own ground.

It was heaven and hell to be in his arms once more. Her hands trembled as they softly touched then hugged his lean hard body to her. His lips left hers and traveled down her throat, then over to nibble gently on one small earlobe before traveling over to her other ear to do the same. She was shaking with reaction, her breasts peaked, her body arched toward his in total surrender. The intimate exploration of his hands sought the slim length of her, sending torrents of emotions she hadn't felt before through her body to compound her dizzying reactions. When he stroked her breast once more she placed her hand over his to still the ever-constant tingling he was bringing to a fever pitch. He held her hand, taking it back to his chest to rub against his own sensitive areas.

"Oh, my Kathleen," he muttered hoarsely, his voice finally giving vent to the anguish of holding her so near, and she trembled once more in answer to his own reaction. "Hold me. Touch me like I touch you. Here. And here." He led her hands on paths she hadn't taken before. And she following willingly.

She was in another world, where the years had dissipated all the loss and sorrow and left just the haunting anticipation of his touch behind. Feelings totally alien to her washed through her body, bringing an ecstasy that only he could assuage. It was better this time. This time she knew the heights they could reach together. The last time she had been a timid virgin, not knowing where the road would lead. But this time . . .

"No!" She suddenly wrenched out of his arms, only now realizing in a heartbreaking second where this tender torture would lead. Hadn't she suffered enough the first time to learn her lesson well? My God, was she insane?

Steve's face was glazed with passion, but within seconds a shutter came down to show the controlled iciness of his soul. "So you're as much a tease today as you were yesterday?" he grated, his breath still heavy. But he held his emotions in check much better than she.

She stared at him, all the vulnerability of her soul shining from her sherry-colored eyes as he continued. "The last time I made you pay up. This time though, I don't think it's worth the trouble. You've been used before, Kathleen—I can tell by your very experienced touch, and I don't care to bother with you. But if I were you, I wouldn't start this again unless you mean to finish. Most men wouldn't stop just because you said to. At least not this far along." He stood, calmly tucking his shirt into the waistband of his jeans. Only his shallow breath gave away the fact that he had been as excited as she.

Her head bent in supplication and shame. Everything that she had used to mold her life had twisted around pretzel-style, making her values seem wasted and her pride without reason. She shivered.

"Don't bother to play the perfect hostess. I'll let myself out."

"Please do. I'm sure it isn't the first time you've played around then had to leave in a hurry." Her shame had disappeared and anger was taking its place. "I've heard that in most 'fun' houses the men take their exit alone. You seem to know the routine well."

"I'm sorry to disappoint you, but I've never had to take that route. There were always willing women." His eyes scanned her golden blond hair, then her softly rounded figure, as if to verify the fact that she had been one of those who had given of themselves. Her cheeks burned a scarlet, her eyes shooting darts under his scrutiny.

Then he was gone.

She pounded the pillows of the couch, tears streaming down her face. Then, finally giving in to the feeling of total desolation, she sobbed. She didn't know when she stopped and lay in the silence, hiccoughing occasionally, but keeping her eyes and ears closed to everything except the scene that had just been played. Once again she had played the fool. In a short span of time her entire way of life had changed. Where once she had lived for her career, scorning men and their more than obvious motives, she was now being consumed and directed by Steve. He was in her life once more and once more he was totally in charge. When would she ever learn?

When the doorbell rang Kathleen started, thinking at first that Steve had returned to taunt her again. But she quickly came to her senses, knowing he would probably elude her for the rest of her stay. He had made it blatantly clear that he wanted nothing to do with her, and in words that held more truth than she would admit.

She hadn't realized the sun had already set and she had been sitting in the room with just the fading fire for light. It must have been at least three hours since Steve had walked out on her.

"Hi. I thought perhaps you had taken a walk. I was just going to ring one more time before I gave up." Merrie stood in the doorway, her eyes crinkling with a pixyish twinkle until she saw the tear marks on Kathleen's face. "Are you all right?" Her concern was Kathleen's undoing. Suddenly Merrie took charge. "Come on," she stated softly, closing the door and leading Kathleen back into the living room.

Merrie put another log on the fire and had a bottle of wine opened and poured within minutes of her arrival. She had turned on a low lamp, which gave

121

out enough light to make the room feel cozy without being a glare to Kathleen's ravished face.

"Now, drink this and relax," Merrie ordered, reaching for the phone and pushing a code of buttons. "Hello, Mrs. Andrews? This is Merrie. Could you send a tray for three to Miss Bolton's cottage? Anything you cook is bound to be delicious. Thanks. Oh, and when the busboy picks up the tray would you tell him to bring the whirling dervish with him? With the trip to his grandmother's delayed a day, he's more hyper than ever!" She chuckled at something the other woman said then hung up.

Merrie walked over and put her hand beneath Kathleen's drink. "Okay, you. Drink up. In half an hour, when Andy comes, you'll wish you were alone again."

Kathleen gave a watery chuckle and did as she was told. The chilled white wine felt good going down, light and very palatable. Just like a wine from Steve's wine cellar should taste.

"Now," Merrie stated in a businesslike tone. "What is all this nonsense about?"

"Just nonsense." Kathleen tried to evade the issue.

But Merrie was emphatic. "Oh, no. I know those tactics well, so don't try to fool me. I want to help." She studied Kathleen, compassion in her eyes. "Won't you let me?" She wiggled deeper into the cushions before reaching for her wineglass. "I'll tell you what. You tell me your secrets then I'll tell you mine."

That brought a smile to Kathleen's lips and they both giggled at the remembered delight of schoolgirl slumber parties where everyone sat around whispering sinful acts. But those days were over for both of them. Kathleen could see just as much heartache in Merrie's eyes as she was sure were in her own.

"It's because of Steve, isn't it?" Merrie's voice was soft with compassion, and at Kathleen's startled expression, the other girl just nodded her head. "I know he was here because he told me not to ring him. He said he'd be in the office later to sign today's correspondence. Besides, I was on my way to my apartment when I saw him leave here." Her wise eyes took in Kathleen's pale cheeks and trembling lips. "And he didn't look much better than you do."

Kathleen turned distant, gulping on her wine and unable to allow Merrie to see anymore. "Hatred does that to you." She stared into the fire, mesmerized by the masculine face that danced in front of her eyes.

"I don't believe it. If anyone has reason to hate, it's Steve, but he's never succumbed to that emotion. Not even with business competitors." She continued her explanation under Kathleen's disbelief. "Oh, he's ruthless, sometimes rude, and always on the overbearing side, but never mean."

"Steve West is jaded, world-weary, and holds as much or more a capacity to hate than you or I could ever fathom." Kathleen stated sadly, hating to break another person's bubble but knowing that she'd seen a side of Steve that Merrie obviously hadn't.

Merrie hesitated a moment, then, as if making up her mind about something, she turned to face Kathleen completely and sat Indian fashion on the couch.

123

"I'm telling tales out of school, but you'll see what I mean about his not hating at the end of my story."

She took a deep breath, staring at the ceiling for a moment, as if finding the proper words with which to start. "Even though Steve was the second male born to his family, he was always the one the others looked to for guidance. His older brother, Ted, couldn't do without his opinions, although he'd get angry or frustrated because he hadn't thought of the solutions himself. He resented Steve because Steve didn't need to rely on others to make his decisions for him."

Kathleen interrupted. "How do you know all this, Merrie? Is this hearsay?" She was intrigued in spite of herself. This wasn't the playboy image that she had seen.

"My husband grew up with Steve's family. They lived in the house, or should I say mansion, next door. When I married Tom I was dragged into that environment and failed in more ways than one. I couldn't live up to the image of what was expected of me." She grimaced at the old memories. "But to make a long story longer, I, too, became caught up with the life of the West family."

"Steve's father was a regular iconoclast, breaking trends and traditions wherever he went in the business world. But what was funny was that he was such a traditionalist at home."

Merrie took a sip of her wine, then continued. "Even though Steve was better qualified to run the business than Ted, Mr. West had to have the older son in power. It was his due, he used to say, and he

124

tried in every way he knew to fit a very round Ted into a very square hole. It never worked. Ted continued to call on Steve to get him out of tight corners he had backed himself into, then resented the fact that Steve *could* come up with the right solutions.

"But the crux of the problem came seven years ago when Steve met and fell in love with a girl named Judith." Merrie saw Kathleen's face lose color but continued anyway, determined to make the beautiful woman understand. "He asked her to marry him, but she demurred, so he took her home to meet 'dear old dad,' and, of course, the rest of the family. And when Ted met her, he finally saw his way to get even. He swept 'poor little Judith' right off her ever-lovin' size sixes and by the next weekend they were married."

"My God!" Kathleen choked.

Merrie nodded her head, her eyes sad with remembrance. "Little Judith instantly saw that she was in touch with the next president of West Enterprises and knew a good thing when she saw it. The witch."

"And Steve?" She didn't really want to know. She really didn't. . . .

"His retaliation was a whirlwind tour of Europe, South America, etcetera. All roads leading from one girl's bed to another. And even though the press was brutal with him, he didn't care. The only thing that ever brought him home was Claire, his little sister. She'd call for him and he'd come running."

"There were other things he could have done besides bed-hop," Kathleen stated bitterly. "He could have stayed and helped Ted."

"And have Judith all over him?" Merrie squeaked

125

incredulously. "Oh, our little Judith wanted the best of both worlds and suddenly wasn't shy enough to sit back and wait. No. The only way Ted was going to win the battle with Judith or business was to learn how to fight it out for himself."

"If that's really what happened, then why is Steve in charge of the company now? What happened to Ted and Judith?"

Merrie reached for the bottle of wine on the low cocktail table, topping off both their glasses before continuing. "Around four years ago everything came to a head. I still don't know the ramifications of it all because I was going through my own tough time. The day after Claire graduated from college, Steve's father died. That same night Ted had an auto accident and broke both legs. When Steve returned home both Ted and Judith accused him of all kinds of things. It seemed old man West had relented at the last moment and wrote a will stating that Steve would be in charge, with Ted below him on the ladder of authority. He must have realized, almost too late, that the company would flounder if Ted had much more to do with it." Merrie rolled her eyes. "And Judith realized that she had married the wrong man after all. She left Ted and filed for divorce. Ted left the family business and began an import-export business of his own, which has turned out to be very successful. Then two years ago Steve began breeding Arabian horses for fun, a kind of business hobby within a business. Now his horses are trained and sent all over the globe, a few even bought and taken back to Argentina, which is really a compliment to Steve's skills."

"Polo. The rich man's game when there's nothing else to do." Kathleen sipped her wine, her mind becoming slightly fuzzy and blurred with the effect. But she didn't want to sharpen her memory. She didn't need to. This afternoon was still in the fore-front of her thoughts.

"Don't knock it till you've tried it, as the expres-sion goes. It's a very stimulating challenge." Merrie laughed. "Even some women play. Just wait until tomorrow. You'll see what I mean." Her smile disap-peared. "But to finish this more than lengthy story and move on to less depressing things," she stated determinedly, ignoring Kathleen's obvious change of subject, "three years ago Judith went back to Ted, totally rejected by Steve. Steve had had his chance to get even with his brother, but he didn't. They now have a daughter, and one on the way. And it's all with Steve's help and understanding."

Merrie stared down at her glass, thoughts of an-other time impressing a sadness upon her face. When she looked up again, tears glistened in her eyes, but her smile was bright. "And so ends the story of the Wests. The point being that even though Ted stole Steve's girl, then made a mess of the company, Steve still tries to help him out. He also still sees Claire quite often and still has time left over to find posi-tions and give help to wayward waifs like me."

"But," Kathleen protested just as the doorbell rang. Merrie jumped to get it, her face lit with the love for the small boy she knew was on the other side.

127

Sure enough, Tim walked in, balancing a tray in one hand and holding the small hand of the impish boy with his other hand. "Mommy, I got three cookies!" Andy held up a chocolate-covered hand clutching dark crumbs of what must have at one time been cookies, his eyes lighting up at the thought of eating the mess. "Hi," he said to Kathleen and she grinned in return, her heart turning over in a flip-flop. He was so darling, dark-headed and gray-eyed, and just the right age to remind her of what she had lost.

"It looks like you have your hand full." Her voice was deep and rasping as she tried to control runaway emotions she didn't want to define.

He nodded his head solemnly. "Mrs. Andrews said I could eat them when I got here." He turned to his mother. "Can I now, Mommy?"

Tim set the full tray down on the desk with a nervous smile, leaving almost as quickly as he had come.

Kathleen was starved and hadn't realized it. She and Merrie both dug into the delicious food, giggling and laughing as if they had been friends for years. It felt good. Kathleen hadn't had a close friend since Sandy, a hundred years ago.

In the middle of eating, Kathleen glanced over at little Andy, sitting by the fireplace, licking the last of the cookies from his hand and seeming to place the crumbs everywhere but in his mouth. "Does he look a lot like your husband, Merrie?" she questioned softly.

Merrie looked startled for a moment, then in a very matter-of-fact voice answered. "Andy isn't

Tom's son, Kathleen. I thought you knew. Tom died six years ago."

"Oh," Kathleen stammered, taken completely by surprise. "I'm sorry . . . I didn't mean to . . . I mean . . ." She blushed at her lack of tact.

Merrie smiled sadly, "Don't feel sorry for me—or Andy. We've built a good life for ourselves, even without a daddy. I'm sorry if I embarrassed you." She turned to her chocolate-covered son. "Come on, honey, time to go home."

And before Kathleen could tell Merrie just how deeply she understood about Andy, how completely she had yearned for an Andy of her own, Merrie and her son were gone.

CHAPTER SIX

It took Kathleen another half bottle of wine to unwind enough to pretend to get ready for sleep. Her eyes wouldn't shut even though she kept telling herself she must rest if she were going to finish this job and leave Steve West's company for good. Her mind tried to rationalize all the reasons she hated him for so long, but her emotions seemed to have their own demands.

Little Andy's face swam in front of her closed eyes, reminding her of one who would have been three and would have looked like that, had he lived. Then she would return from that small portion of her mind, telling herself she was imagining things. Steve couldn't possibly be Andy's father, or Merrie would have said so. Besides, Merrie seemed to look on Steve as more of a brother than a lover.

Then once more she would sink into a light, disturbing sleep, only to wake quickly, with a jerk.

In the middle of the night her body still craved the touch of Steve's hands against her heated flesh. Her body still remembered the afternoon and the pitch of excitement she had felt that had not been assuaged. Her hips would not obey her unspoken command to rest quietly, but shifted to find the coolness of the sheets as she lay staring at the darkened light fixture and told herself she was crazy. But still she could feel the touch of his cool lips on the warmth of her softly mounded breasts, the feather-light touch of his hands as they caressed her waist, only to move down and slowly skim her thighs, generating a pulsating heat within her. His warm breath fanned across her neck and shoulders only to tease the already erect nipple over her quickly beating heart. She moved again, her hips responding to her mood, only to be stilled when she silently commanded them quiet.

So now another piece of the puzzle was slipped into place. Steve didn't come after her because of his father's death and his subsequent taking over of the business. Small consolation that he had had a valid excuse, for he probably wouldn't have come after her anyway.

She sat up in the darkness. What was the matter with her? She had tried to run away from him, never planning to see him again. So why was she so relieved to know he had been tied up with personal problems? Why did she want to believe he'd needed an excuse not to follow her? The answer came straight and clear. For all those years she had hoped against hope, secretly wanting him to care enough to follow and claim her. She had continued to want him, to desire him, to imagine being taken by him as she had been that one silvery, moon-drenched night.

"No!" Her voice whispered in the silent darkness. She clutched the sheet against her bare breasts, her heart thumping loudly in her ears as the discovery that shouldn't have surprised her, did. She had been kidding herself for years. She still desired him, and what was worse was she wanted him to desire her, to stay awake nights wanting the pressure of her body next to his, the taste of her mouth, the softness of her pliable flesh under his hands, the pressure of her breasts against his hard, masculine body. Nothing had changed.

She threw aside the sheet and stood, wiping away an errant tear that traveled her cheek, the only outward display of her emotional turmoil. She walked through the bedroom and into the small but perfect living room to stop at the large window overlooking the woods. There was a light powdering of snow on the ground, but her body had a fine sheen of wetness on it, as if she had been inside a tepid sauna. The full moon shimmered down on the tall pines, silhouetting them against the smoky gray clouds that occasionally scuttled by. She wrapped her arms around her heated body and focused her eyes on a midnight dark spot far away as her mind played tricks on her and conjured up Steve's face, laughing and warm in the early morning sunlight. He'd been so reachable this morning, and she'd rebuffed him, placing the strain

between them once more. It was her fault. It was
. . .

A gray-black shadow moved by the edge of the
trees and the soft hair on Kathleen's arms rose as
adrenaline poured through her system to eliminate
the relaxing effect of the wine. Without seeing anything but the barest outline of a shape, every vibrant
nerve in her body aimed its sensors toward Steve. He
stepped into the muted moonlight and she could see
the bulky fleece of his heavy sheepskin jacket. Silver-
dappled moonbeams glistened off the damp snow-
flakes that landed on carelessly combed jet black
hair.

They stared at each other for what seemed eons
before he slowly moved toward her, his eyes holding
her in total suspension. He took the steps one measured foot at a time. And she waited, her unclad body
bathed in moonlight as she stood in front of the large
bay window and waited for him to come to her. He
reached the glimmering sheet of glass, gazing at her
through the misty pane as if it weren't there at all.
She stared back, devouring him with her eyes, realizing he wore jeans and a coat, but no shirt. He, too,
had been too tense and restless to sleep. He nodded
his head as if answering her unspoken question, then
slowly reached toward the large pane, his finger hesitantly outlining her slim body in the mist that hung
gently on the window. His eyes bore into hers, sending definite erotic messages that her pliant body re-
sponded to at once. His gaze traveled the length of
her, halting at the firm feminine indentation of her
waist, the soft swelling of her abdomen, the V where

133

her thighs pressed together. Her hands, curled at her sides, itched to touch his skin in return. For he was stroking her with his velvet gray eyes, seeing more of her than she had ever allowed a man to see.

Suddenly his hand on the window ceased its sensuous travels. He continued to stare at her form outlined in the pale moonlight, caressing her with his very presence. Her blood sang through already fired veins, settling in the nerve center of her abdomen, aching for fulfillment only he could truly give her. She felt poised on the brink of that ecstasy, waiting for a sign, any sign, from him. A small, sad smile tugged at the corners of his mouth and he slowly shook his head no. He took two fingers and touched his mouth, then the glass between them. Then he turned and walked with measured steps back the way he had come, only to disappear into the shadows of the tall trees, leaving behind a taunting ghost of himself to haunt Kathleen's mind and body.

She watched his retreating shadow, wanting to stop him from leaving but unable to do so. She stood until the silver path of the moon traveled out of her sight and the chill air finally claimed her senses. Then, as if in a trance, she walked back to her bed and covered her naked body with the sheet, closing her eyes and finally allowing sleep to claim her with its peace.

"You'll enjoy the horses once you get used to them," Merrie assured Kathleen as they strolled along the tree-lined paths, stopping and opening each cottage door as they went to give Kathleen a better idea of what each kitchen needed. There was a slight strain between the two women today, though neither acknowledged its cause. Merrie continued to chatter, covering up the silences. "And watching a polo game is really a thrill! I didn't think I'd ever get caught up in something like that, but it gets in your blood."

They had finished touring the cottages and finally edged toward the barns and fields. The broad expanse of field had to be three times the size of a football field. The grass was dead for the winter, but snow had not been allowed to cover the white markings on the ground. It was clear from the echos that rang through the air that the teams were getting ready to play a game.

Within seconds six men wearing dark blue polo shirts with skin-tight khaki pants appeared on tall, proud horses. They galloped across the ground, small hard hats on their heads and long slim mallets in their hands as they made a smooth swing to hit at the white ball that rolled swiftly with each hit.

"Normally they play in teams of four, but for practice they take what they can get and divide up the number of men to make it even. When you see the game next week, you'll understand even more." Merrie's voice was low so as not to disturb the players or the horses as they stomped themselves warm in the chilly early morning air. The large, magnificent Thoroughbreds blew smoke from their nostrils, their heads waving impatiently as they waited for the rider's commands. Suddenly the ball was in motion again and the pulsing thunder of hooves beat against the near-frozen ground as the sound rang through the air. The sharp crack and the whistling sound of the ball melded together to send excitement racing through Kathleen's veins.

She tensed as she waited for the next hit, then tensed again, and again. The players were fast and expert, all seeming to know what the other riders were doing and how their strategy would work. Crack! And the ball rose just above the ground to skim through the air toward one of the two goals at either end of the field. Crack! And another rider blocked it before turning his horse completely around and galloping with the wind toward the other end of the field.

Two riders went after the same ball, knees almost touching as they practically flew by. Mallets were raised in the air and Kathleen held her breath as she watched, realizing they could hit each other and be seriously hurt. She watched in horror as she realized one of the riders was Steve. The other, a short, much darker man, gracefully swung his mallet under the horse's neck to gain the prize from his opponent, earning a low curse for his efforts. A smile split his face before he wheeled about and rode hard toward his goal.

Both women stood and watched the game, each deep in her own thoughts as the action continued in front of them. But when the whistle called for a break, they turned simultaneously and walked away slowly.

"Like I said," Merrie continued as if never having

stopped the conversation, "it's an exciting sport, but one that gets me tensed every time I see it."

"I can see why," Kathleen muttered, trying to cover her own emotions with gruffness. "Don't they ever get hurt?"

"Oh, yes. The game isn't without dangers, most of them very real. The trick is to pretend that everything will be all right, whether it will be or not."

"Do they play every day?"

"Every chance they get. I think it's sort of like a race car driver behind a beautiful car. Whether he's on the track or not, he's got to see what an engine can do. Even when these guys are riding the range, they're thinking polo and how to make the horse do what they want, making moves, scoring goals." Merrie laughed nervously. "Almost like life is to them."

"Just one big challenge."

"Something like that. Carlos"—Merrie turned to grin impishly—"that's the guy who took the goal from Steve. Well, he's from Argentina and will be managing here as soon as Steve has everything set up the way he wants."

"Why here?"

"Argentina is the leader in polo. If someone poor wants to get ahead and loves horses, they find a rich patron to sponsor them in polo. Here we treat it more like a joke, or at best a rich man's hobby. In Argentina it's taken seriously."

"And is that how Carlos got here, by being sponsored?"

"In a way." Merrie hesitated. "Carlos comes from a middle class family much like mine, but horses are

137

in his blood. He believes in them much as we would believe in motherhood, the flag, and so forth."

Kathleen noted a certain restraint in her voice. "And is that bad?"

Merrie gave a nervous chuckle. "Only if it becomes your life-style." Her voice held a tinge of sadness. "And sometimes I think Carlos cares more for regimentation and horses than anything else."

"Do I detect a romance?" Kathleen teased before she saw the shininess of Merrie's eyes. She clasped the other woman's arm in sympathy, her own heart knowing the ache of loving the wrong man.

"It's not what you think. Carlos has asked to marry me, but he's so damn autocratic! He lives by some schedule implanted in his head at birth, and with the exception of taking chances on the polo field, he is as straight and stuffy as anyone can possibly be!"

The soft thudding of hooves interrupted their conversation and they turned to watch two riders bearing down on them, horses riding fast and eating up the ground before coming to a smart stop just in front of them.

Kathleen's hunger for Steve showed in her eyes, and by the soft dark look in his, they were both thinking of last night and the silent, almost awesome communication they had held in the moonlight.

"Where are you going?" His voice was low and husky, his hand reaching out to touch her cheek and the curve on the side of her face.

"Back to work. Merrie was just trying to explain

138

some of the merits of polo to a novice." Her voice was breathless.

His eyes crinkled in the corners as he smiled slowly, a secret message passing through his hand to her skin. "I'll be at your cabin at twelve for a sandwich. Be there."

"And what kind of sandwich do you want, master?" she teased, intimately scanning the long lean length of him as he sat in the saddle of the proud stallion. There was no thought of refusal in her mind.

"You know what I want, my Kathleen. I'll have the restaurant deliver something for us to eat." He sat up straight again, wheeling his horse around to head back toward the field. "Just be there."

It wasn't until after he had thundered off with the man called Carlos fast behind him that Kathleen realized she had not been introduced. Somehow the men had come between Kathleen and Merrie, separating them for the two different conversations. The women looked at each other, realizing the error, then began giggling in understanding.

There was no rush. They would all meet another time. Something else niggled at the back of Kathleen's mind, but she shoved it away as she and Merrie walked companionably back toward her cabin. This wasn't the time for problems. Not today. Not today.

Although it was almost ten when she had seen Steve on the field, twelve didn't come soon enough. Kathleen checked the small cottage, straightening things that had already been straightened, putting things down only to pick them up once again. She checked to make sure the wood box was filled, the wine cooling, the fire blazing, the bath towels neatly hung. And all the while she relived the almost dreamlike quality of their meeting last night. Every time she thought of Steve her stomach tightened in anticipation and she had to stop whatever she was doing for a few minutes.

When the doorbell finally rang she was almost faint with relief. But opening the door only tightened her nerves more, for he stood in the entrance and the sight of him made her heart pound with anticipation.

His gaze swept the room only to return to her slight form as she shivered in the cold blast of air. He closed the door quietly but quickly before shedding his sheepskin jacket on the floor and swooping her into the intimate hold of his arms to share his warmth and generate more. Neither said a word as lips joined in a deeply searching kiss that told everything there was to tell. When he finally allowed her room to breathe she had to hold on to his waist, her shaking fingers tucked into the belt at his slim hips to keep her balance. They walked side by side into the living area, not stopping until they reached the same section of window they had stood at the night before.

"I thought I wanted to see you so badly last night that I dreamed you up." His voice was low and husky, almost a whisper as he stared down at her, his hands on her waist tightening as if he were afraid she would disappear. "I thought you were my own special ghost who would haunt me and me only."

Her hand strayed to his temples, fingertips running through the velvet darkness of his hair that was slightly shaded with silver. "Then why didn't you come in? I wanted you to."

"Because I was afraid you'd vanish and I wouldn't be able to find you."

"I never went anywhere you weren't able to follow." Her lips reached up to trail the contours of his throat, filling her nostrils with his own special scent, tickled by the mat of hair at the base of his throat.

"Yes, you did," he muttered before his lips once more claimed hers in a kiss that was more a searing brand than something born out of passion. His arms enfolded her close to his length and she could feel the need of him pulsating just as she could feel her own passion building to a rising pitch.

"Don't run off again, my Kathleen. I won't let you. You were meant to be here, close to me." His low, rough voice was filled with heavy emotions and lulled her into accepting his words at first, then his meaning slowly became clear. He wanted her there as his mistress, his plaything. Someone to come to when nature's base instincts called. A receptacle . . .

The bell rang before Kathleen could complete her thoughts and Steve muttered an oath before making a move to answer it.

Tim's wide, boyish eyes were even wider as he followed Steve's angry footsteps back into the room, setting down the covered tray and beating a hasty path back out and into the newly fallen snow.

"Damn it, I told Merrie to send this over an hour ago," he muttered under his breath, looking much like a petulant child.

141

She chuckled, bringing his startled gray gaze back to her, his expression appreciating her laughter. His eyes crinkled in the corners and he looked sheepish for just a moment before leading her over to the couch and sitting her in front of the fire.

"Okay, okay, so I'm impatient. But you knew that already. Now sit here and I'll bring your meal to you." He moved lithely, picking up the tray and setting it on the low coffee table before grabbing a bottle of wine from the refrigerator and sweeping up two wineglasses from the shelf.

"You don't have to do this, you know," she murmured, her eyes overflowing with tenderness.

"Oh, yes, I do if I'm going to keep you happy. And I want you staying around for a while." Again she felt an ache as he referred to her so casually, but her bright smile hid it well.

"In that case, serve on!"

"Just don't get used to this kind of service. I do other things better than serving lunches," he teased, delighted at watching a peach color tinge her cheeks.

"And you didn't even put this one together. Shame on you for taking credit. So far all I've seen you do is carry a tray and open a bottle of wine. Big deal." He placed a plate, filled with hot spicy chicken, potato salad, and fresh green beans in her lap.

"That's the option of the boss. If I get the credit you can't fault me because I also have to take the blame when something goes wrong." He leaned over and brushed her lips with a chaste kiss before reaching for his own plate. "Now eat, because I have other

142

things I'd rather do with my time than chew on chicken."

"Such as?" She munched on a leg, savoring the taste of the spices. She hadn't realized she was so hungry. The walk this morning must have worked up an appetite. His eyes gleamed with hidden meaning.

"Such as nibble on your luscious neck." He tore a big bite of his own helping, making a hungry face as he did so. The silence was deafening as they stared at each other, each sensing the almost desperate physical and emotional need of the other. They stood slowly, suddenly forgetting their hunger for food as they realized their true hunger. Steve held out his hand to Kathleen, palm upturned and open, and she trustingly slipped her hand into his, not hesitating to give what his eyes said he wanted.

In a short time they were in the bedroom, each taking time in unbuttoning the other's shirt. Her hands stroked across his hairy chest and then moved down to his belt and the zipper of his jeans, caressing the skin beneath as she unfastened his clothing. He, too, took his time, savoring with his lips and hands every small patch of flesh he exposed to his gaze.

"God, you're lovely. So soft," he muttered hoarsely, and she couldn't answer. She didn't have a voice to tell him how marvelously hard his skin was beneath her palm, how sharply contoured his muscles felt.

Finally they were completely undressed, standing face-to-face, commemorating the flesh beneath their touch as they explored each other's trembling bodies. His hands traveled down her sides, then crossed to

143

reach and hold her hands, leading her to the bed. She pulled down the spread to expose the softness of the blanket but got no further. His body was behind hers, molding himself to her sweet, full curves. He cupped the roundness of her breasts swinging free, his thumbs drawing lazy circles around each peaked and hardened nipple. Her breath caught in her throat and a weakness made her legs tremble before he drew her down and turned her around on the flat plane of the bed, staring into her soul with eyes narrowed in determination.

"You're mine, Kathleen. Do you understand? You're mine," he repeated in a voice that was ragged with a fierceness that sent a shiver down her spine. Then he was with her, his legs pinning her to the warmth of the blanket. "Mine." He nuzzled her slim neck, his beard rasping in delicious torment against her smooth skin.

His mouth tasted like fresh cool wine, his scent was completely male, his skin a rough, firm texture. Kathleen never wanted him to stop touching her, never wanted him to let her go. She loved the feel of his muscled arms beneath her hands, the feel of his ribs covered with taut skin, and a shiver went through her as he began the same exploratory path on her own softened curves. She reveled in it. She wanted to be his more than anything she had ever wanted. The desire for him was stronger than any rational thoughts or feelings she might have had in the past. A throbbing ache filled her marrow and flames of silver and gold licked through her ready body as he took even greater liberties, molding her, turning her, positioning her to fit his curves and contours. Their breaths were short, light gasps, hands searching, eyes open to watch and reveal the wondrous feelings they aroused in each other. There was an urgent thrust of skin to skin, and they wished one could sink into the other, as lovers over and over have always wished.

"Do you want me, my Kathleen? Do you? You have to tell me. Tell me," he muttered against the curve of her breast.

"Yes," she whispered. "Yes."

When he brought her to the peak of sensation, Kathleen could feel tears slide down her cheeks to plop upon the pillow below, as a release so sweet flooded her being. He shivered once more, groaned her name as in a litany, and collapsed his full weight upon her.

They both fell asleep within minutes, arms and legs entwined as if to insure that neither would leave without the other waking. The restless night before had taken its toll on them, and with release came exhaustion. An hour later they awoke to begin the joyous ceremony once more.

It was a dark gray sky that greeted them when they finally resumed the now cold meal. They built the fire once more, sipped the wine, and ate the chicken, tasting nothing but feeling exuberantly happy. They swapped stories of growing up and the crazy silly things children do. They grinned, touched, and sat in the peace of their surroundings, for the first time totally relaxed. Both had slipped into jeans, but neither wore a top and there was no embarrassment in the fact. It was as if they were the only two people on earth.

Suddenly Steve's smoky gray eyes turned serious. He searched for an answer when Kathleen wasn't sure of his question. He looked sad, almost regretful as he took her slim form in, as if branding it. "I meant what I said earlier, Kathleen. You're mine." His voice was low, mellow, with a hint of possessiveness. "I don't care who was before or who was after as long as there will be no one else from here on."

"Does the same go for you, Steve?" she questioned quietly, trying not to beg for the answer she wanted but holding her breath just the same.

"The same goes for me." It was a statement of fact. He pushed away the light tendrils of hair from her ear, caressing her cheek as he did so.

"Promise?" she teased huskily, only not really teasing.

"Promise." His wine-cooled lips met hers to seal their bargain and she relaxed against him, breast to chest, as she felt the tender security of his arms.

They made love again that night before falling into a deep sleep.

The gray dawn slanted through the window, chasing dustbeams across the room. Kathleen woke to a soft kneading of her breast. She turned slightly, allowing Steve greater access to what he seemed to so enjoy touching. She watched his face through her lowered lids. His eyes were still closed and a small, contented smile made the corners of his mouth rise.

"Mmm, I love finding you in the palm of my hand

146

when I wake up," he mumbled as he turned on his side to fit her to his own curves.

"And I love being here," she answered back, her own hands busy exploring the territory she had only learned last night.

"You'd better, for this is where you're staying."

Kathleen chuckled. "Ben would surely be surprised at my new working conditions," she retorted saucily, receiving a pinch on her bottom for her answer.

They came together slowly, leisurely, enjoying the non-hectic movements of their lovemaking. Kathleen watched Steve smile through it all, never realizing just how jaunty her own private grin was. . . .

CHAPTER SEVEN

She was buoyant as she made her way to the restaurant later the next day. Steve had left just after dawn's light. They both had work to do, he said, and she knew he was right. The business world didn't stop just because two people fell in love.

She knew it was love on her part, but she could only hope it was love on his part too. He had never said the word, but surely his actions showed how much he cared for her. Perhaps in time she would be able to show him her commitment and in exchange he would do the same. But not yet. Not yet.

She almost giggled as she made her way over the bridge and toward the entrance of the lodge. Two weeks ago and she would have sooner spit in his face than talk to him. Yet, here she was, planning to be a mistress to the very man she had sworn to hate. But that wasn't true. She had blamed him for something

148

she knew she shouldn't have. It had taken two to form the mess she had made of her life four years ago. And only now could she admit it to herself. Only now that she had found him again did she realize just how much blame she had put on his shoulders. But all that would change now.

The dining room was filled with workers, promotion people, and a few of the newspaper interviewers. In one month the polo club would be stabling members' horses and in another it would be open to the public, at least the public that was interested and wealthy enough to pay the price.

Merrie saw Kathleen first and stood waving her arms to attract her attention. Relieved at the other woman's friendly gesture, Kathleen weaved her way through the tables to seat herself next to Steve's secretary and the man she had called Carlos. They sat at a table by the long windows overlooking the pond.

"I saw you coming down the path. You sure seem in a good mood," Merrie teased after formally introducing Carlos as the manager of the polo club. Her eyes had a sparkle as she took in the chocolate-brown wool slacks and form-fitting sweater Kathleen wore. She looked so cool and sophisticated. The perfect match for Steve.

Carlos was a wit, but his eyes spoke only to Merrie, who tried very hard to ignore his smoldering stare. She looked flustered and excited and yet something was making her withdraw from the small party. When Andy came running up to demand his favorite dessert, ice cream, the table suddenly became silent.

"I think the boy has had his share," Carlos stated firmly. "After all, this is supposed to be breakfast."

Merrie's chin came up. "And I believe he can have another bowl. Ice cream doesn't have harmful side effects."

"No, but giving in to a child's whims is harmful. And you give in to him all the time."

"He's my child."

"No one else would have him in a few years. He'll be too spoiled." Carlos's voice was tinged with disgust.

Kathleen watched in almost open-mouthed wonder as the two argued, neither giving an inch. Andy continued to whine, tapping his mother's arm as he did so. Silently Kathleen stood and took Andy's hand, leading the way toward the kitchen. While those two argued, she would take care of the small child.

"Please give him some ice cream, Tim, would you?"

"Yes, ma'am, I was supposed to, but I didn't know he finished eating."

"Where's his plate?" Kathleen questioned, finding the answer on the back table even before Tim pointed to it. She turned slowly toward the little boy. He looked sheepish but determined.

"I thought you told your mommy that you had finished everything on your plate."

He nodded his head, finding his finger better to chew on than words.

"I'll tell you what, Andy. If you do what you said you were going to do and eat your meal, then Tim will do what he's supposed to do and give you ice cream," she stated quietly but firmly. "Is that a deal?"

Again the small boy nodded his head, his voice still not returning. He looked so forlorn Kathleen bent down and gave him a swift hug.

"Handled very nicely. Are you studying for motherhood?" Steve's teasing voice hit a nerve and she jumped. "Or trying to keep the peace between Carlos and Merrie?"

Her eyes rounded. "How did you know?"

His eyes glinted with hidden laughter. "I've been in that hotseat enough myself. Carlos believes Andy should have a strong hand and Merrie isn't ready to give it."

"I see," Kathleen said slowly. "I think."

Steve laughed. "Me too, I think." His arm wrapped around her slim shoulders, sending a feeling of shared warmth through her as he walked her back into the dining room and toward the table where Merrie and Carlos sat glowering at each other. If nothing else, she and Steve could keep the conversational ball rolling.

When the meal was over and Kathleen was nursing her last cup of coffee before returning to the various cottages to work, Steve leaned over and took her hand in his. He rubbed his thumb along her quickening pulse.

"I'll be tied up again this afternoon, but I'll see you late this evening," he murmured for her ears alone.

151

"What time?" Her voice sounded breathless, her eyes sparkled.

"Around eleven or so. Keep the homefires burning." His dark gray eyes held a multitude of hidden meanings and she glanced down at their entwined fingers, peach tingeing her cheeks as she nodded her head. Only Steve had the ability to destroy her already unsteady equilibrium and cause her emotions to swirl like a small dust cloud.

The afternoon sped by. Kathleen had worked out color schemes for four of the cottages, including her own, and was pleased with her work. If he wanted quality, he was certainly getting it! She grinned when she thought of the bill to come. He could never say he was short-changed when it came to original work, for she had outdone herself.

By four o'clock she had done most of what she had set herself as the goal for the day. In fact she had room for one more cabin before calling it quits and beginning on the paperwork.

She whistled an old children's tune as she walked out of one cottage and locked the door behind her. She was making her way to the next one when she realized someone was farther along on the same path. Carlos's grin was endearing and somehow sad as he halted, waiting for her to join him.

"I thought I heard someone behind me," he smiled. "And since no one I know whistles, I knew it had to be you." He took her arm and they strolled along.

She was surprised he was here. Not long ago she had heard the dull thundering of horses hooves and thought he and Steve were playing polo on the large field. "Where are you headed?"

"I'm just taking a walk and trying to come up with some answers that will appease my melancholy Latin mind."

"Melancholy? I would never have called you that, Carlos."

His steps slowed even more, bringing them to an almost halting pace on the brick walkway between the two sheltered cottages. "Ah, but the Latin mind is never completely happy, Miss Bolton. We are fatalists, are we not? And I have reason to be depressed. The one I love can't seem to make up her mind about our relationship. Consequently she is always running away from what should be to what is easiest."

"We're discussing Merrie?" she hazarded, wondering what else could have happened. Now that she and Steve were together she wanted everyone to be happy.

Carlos's dark Spanish eyes were troubled. "I love her very much and I believe she loves me. But the bone of contention turns out to be a small child of four—Andy. I would be a good father to him, I already care for the boy, but I will not allow him to be spoiled." His expression turned grim. "In this world there is no longer a space for spoiled children. They must learn some sort of guidelines before they go out into the world. Andy has yet to have any form of discipline."

"Andy is just a little boy, Carlos," Kathleen said.

"And Merrie dotes on him no more than any other single parent."

Carlos gave a rueful grin. "Are you saying that I'm the jealous one who needs to be disciplined?"

"Of course not." She smiled, giving his hand a quick hug to soften her words. "But perhaps there is room for a compromise?"

Carlos sighed heavily then leaned over and placed a chaste kiss on her forehead. "You are right, perhaps there is." His grin changed the somberness of his expression. "And now I know why I usually hear giggles and laughter whenever I see you and Merrie together. You are both sweet and gentle-natured." A glitter lit up his dark eyes and she smiled at his observation.

She thought of the businessmen she had had to deal with in one way or the other in the past four years, and chuckled. She doubted if they could see a gentle side of her, even though she knew it existed. "Not always, Carlos. Even with the ones we love," she stated softly.

An hour later Kathleen was deep into her catalogues, wondering what on earth could give a drab green and white kitchen charm. When the front door slammed on the cottage, she thought it was Merrie, and called out.

"I'm in the kitchen, Merrie, doing what I do best! Nothing!"

"That wasn't always true, my Kathleen." Steve's voice held a note of laughter, but it seemed forced. She turned to see sharp gray eyes almost physically probing her and a feeling of wrongdoing invaded her.

She shook it off, giving him a bright smile that showed her true feelings for him. What was the sense in disguising them?

"And what brings you to this part of the complex? I thought you were going to be busy all day."

"And I thought you were busy too."

Her brows went up in surprise. "I'll have you know that even though I look like I'm doing nothing, my mind is busily working away trying to come up with a color combination to match this drab kitchen. Why? What are you hinting at?"

"Nothing," he replied as his eyes hungrily roamed her figure. He looked like the panther ready to devour his first meal of the week. Then he moved with the swiftness of that animal to pull her into his arms. His lips came down in a bruising kiss to steal the breath from her. His hands roughly traveled the length of her body, pulling her toward his lean, firm maleness. There was a hurried movement about him, as if he wanted to throw her down on the carpeted floor and rape her, hurt her. She soothed the back of his neck, his shoulders, trying to slow him down. She wasn't frightened, but neither was she aroused. His hands brought her close to him, suddenly hurting as they scraped against her tender skin. It wasn't right. He was making her feel like an object, a sordid, tattered, kept woman. Surely no woman who was loved would be treated this way!

She pushed with all her might but not until he was finished did he relinquish his hold on her, allowing a little room to come between them.

"What's the matter, my Kathleen? Aren't you in the mood?"

"Not to be mauled," she stated emphatically, wiping her hand against the tenderness of her lips.

"Oh, really? I've tried being gentle and that didn't work. What does it take for me to reach and open that small part of yourself that remains aloof, even in passion? The part that always seems to be locked away, like a secret in a dark attic?"

"What secrets? What part of myself have I withheld from you?"

A darkness shuttered down on his eyes before he turned his back to her. Picking up the catalogue on the counter, Steve began leafing through the pages.

She was confused. How could he feel a withdrawal from her when she didn't even realize she was withdrawing? It didn't matter that there was a nagging voice in the back of her mind that told her she was holding back a portion of herself. Just one small portion that could be used to cloak her in dignity if she needed it. One small part of her brain that told her she hadn't completely allowed herself to succumb to his potent brand of magic.

Steve watched her face turn into a mask of blankness. His shoulders stiffened, then he turned, anger and frustration blazing from his smoky gray eyes before the anger seemed to slowly disappear and be replaced with self-derision.

"I'm sorry," he sighed. "It's been a rough day, and I guess I took it out on you." He smiled and suddenly the sun was shining in all its glory. "Forgive me?" His hand traced her jawline, cupped her chin, then

156

moved down to rest on her shoulder and give a slight squeeze. "Hmmm?"

"You can't seem to make up your mind, Steve. Either you ignore me when I invite you into my cottage, shaking your head with regret, or you spend the night with me, or manhandle me. I don't like the mood shifts you seem to go through."

"It's no different from blowing first hot and then cold, Kathleen, which is what you do." His eyes once more sparked with anger. His confusion was genuine, as was his accusation. He was as frustrated with her as she with him! Only he knew exactly how he felt . . . and she didn't. Where did she fit in his life? What part was she supposed to play?

Kathleen's stomach churned at the obvious answer. No matter how much she tried, she knew she would miss his lovemaking, his touch, his body, when he finally tired of her and asked her to leave. Suddenly Kathleen needed air.

"If you'll excuse me, I'll trot on to the next cottage," she mumbled as she tried to squeeze through the doorway sideways.

"Kathleen!" Steve's voice was a bullet shot in the now quiet room. She continued to walk toward the cottage door. "Kathleen!" he called again and still she continued. She quietly shut the door on Steve's harsh words.

She ate alone that night, taking a quiet corner in the restaurant before it was even partially filled. Kathleen was assured that the food was delicious, but it all tasted like bland sawdust to her. Over and over in her mind was the roughness of Steve's kisses,

157

the challenging look in his eyes. And then her stomach would clench into another small knot. There would always be other women for a man like Steve. Right now he was intrigued with her because she presented a mystery to be unraveled. But he could never stay faithful to one woman. It wasn't in him. When she had made the pact with herself to stay by him she hadn't realized how hard it would be to live with a man who didn't love her!

"Why such a long face, señorita? Has something gone wrong?" Carlos stood by her table, a brandy glass in his hand.

She gave a wan smile. "No, I'm just enjoying the scenery, Carlos." She glanced around. "Where's Merrie?"

"She's in the kitchen. Little Andy pulled a bread tray down on his head." At Kathleen's concerned look he rested a comforting hand on her shoulder. "No, no, he is all right. It's the bread that has a problem. He sat on half the loaves so he could cry in comfort."

They chuckled, each seeing the comic picture in their minds.

"He can find more things to get into," Carlos continued, staring into his golden-hued brandy. "You can tell he's a West through and through."

Kathleen's face drained white as she heard her suspicions being confirmed. "What?" she croaked, her voice freezing in her throat.

Carlos glanced down at her, surprised. "You did not know? I'm sorry, I thought Merrie had discussed it with you. You both seemed so close."

158

"Excuse me," she whispered as she rose from her chair and, leaving most of her food untouched, walked stiffly toward the exit. She had to get to her cabin before she would collapse. She didn't want anyone to see the misery that was so apparent in her brown eyes. Just before she reached the arched doorway, she saw Steve and Deborah standing in it. He was wearing a midnight black tuxedo that fit his body as if tailor-made. Deborah wore a black sequined dress that hugged every luscious curve of her body. They made a striking couple.

In Kathleen's bitterness she realized just how Steve and the actress deserved each other. Rattlesnakes traveled in twos, didn't they? She was the odd man out, not them.

Inside she began to laugh hysterically at her own poorly made joke. After all, it wasn't Deborah's fault that Steve didn't care enough for Kathleen. But her eyes froze over as they locked with Steve's. All she could glean from his expression was undisguised triumph. But what he had won, beside totally humiliating her, she didn't know.

His glance swung back to Deborah, warming like a spring flower, reinforcing Kathleen with the fact that she had merely been a fill-in for his base instincts. The hurt was almost unbearable, but her pride came to her rescue as she sidestepped them and walked through the large lobby toward the front door.

"Kathleen!" Carlos's voice whipped across the almost deserted space and she could hear his quick footsteps as he followed her. By the time he reached

159

her side she was already walking out the door. "You forgot your coat, my friend, and the temperature is dropping rapidly. You will catch your death. . . ."

"Thank you, Carlos." She turned, allowing him to drape the heavy jacket on her slim shoulders. As he silently nodded and held open the outer door for her, she glanced once more at the entrance of the restaurant, only to see Steve's face as he watched them both.

She left quickly, not even feeling the cold as she hurried down the darkened path toward her cottage, and her own private haven. Once she closed the door on the world the tears began. She cried most of the evening before finally conceding defeat and allowing herself the dignity of showering and then sitting in front of the fire with a small glass of chilled wine. Her mind was empty of thoughts now. Her emotions had been placed back in a deep freeze where they had been the past four years, and would stay, never to be brought out to inflame the heat of passion or the pain of rejection again.

The doorknob turned roughly back and forth as if having a life of its own. Kathleen stood and walked to the small hall, watching with hypnotic fascination as the knob was pushed and pulled, turned and jiggled.

"Open this door, damn it!" Steve's voice came loud and clear through the hardwood, his voice a growl that would have put fear in most hearts. But not Kathleen's. She had cloaked herself in immunity.

"Go away, Steve. There's nothing for you here,"

Kathleen stated with deadly calm, and the doorknob stopped its twisting.

"Let me in, Kathleen, or I'll go back and get the master key. You can't keep me out."

"If you come in here, then I'll leave in the morning." Her voice was calm, too matter-of-fact for him to doubt.

"You're mine, Kathleen. I told you that early in the game."

"Only for as long as I wanted to be. I've changed my mind. Now I belong to me again." She watched with detached fascination as the doorknob stopped its dance.

"There is no going back." His voice was low and still held a bit of a threat. She sipped the wine from her glass.

"How right you are, Mr. West," she said quietly, retracing her steps to the couch to stare into the fire once more and sip her quickly warming wine. No one could go back, only forward, and onto a path they had chosen that was tried and true. Chosen because they could not get hurt. Paths that were familiar and comfortable, with no thought of up-and-down see-saw emotions. Safe was the operative word.

Her subconscious registered his booted feet leaving, almost muffled with the newly fallen snow, and her lips curved into a small, sad smile before her brown eyes once more gazed at the fire in hopes of drowning out the pain forever.

He had made love to her, left her pregnant, and then went on to make love to Merrie and do the same. Only Merrie was more forgiving than she

161

could ever be. Merrie allowed him to watch Andy grow without anger or hurt from the past, while Kathleen couldn't begin to imagine the hurt involved if her own beautiful little boy had survived and she had watched him grow into the image of a man she hated. The thought hurt so much it was as if a knife was in her belly, twisting and turning from the deceit of it all. Her hand clenched at her stomach, as once more she felt the physical anguish of the night she lost the child. . . .

"Kathleen!" Steve stood on the back deck, his eyes flaring with anger and frustration. "Open this door now!"

She turned and confronted him through the glass, remembering another, more tender time she had done so and he had walked away. There should be no more walking away for either of them until they had talked and ended this relationship once and for all. Besides, it was useless to deny him entrance. She might as well get it over with. Whatever had been growing between them should be severed now, before it was too late.

She was totally calm and in control when she ushered him into the room. As far as she was concerned, the fates had already decreed the outcome of this discussion.

He stepped into the room, glancing about as if he hoped to find tangible evidence of someone or something that could make her change her mind and personality so quickly. He wanted to place the blame for this new quirk in their relationship elsewhere, but could find nothing.

He gave a heavy sigh. She had returned to stand in front of the fire, her eyes reflecting the dancing flames that she stared into. He reached out to bring her back closer to him. She stiffened.

"What is it, darling? Is it Deborah? Is that it? I couldn't very well tell the woman that I never wanted to see her again without seeing her again." Kathleen could feel him trying to wheedle her out of a bad mood, much like a child who couldn't have a treat she especially wanted is offered a replacement. "She was only here on business anyway."

"It doesn't matter that she was with you. The problem is me." Kathleen stared up at him, her eyes blurred with tears and wine and heartache. "I want you to leave me alone. Let me live my life without you turning me inside out all the time."

His eyes showed his apology even before he uttered it. "Are you still angry about four years ago? Is that what this is all about?" Steve's voice was low and soothing. A small smile tugged at the corners of his mouth, confirming the fact that he still didn't understand what their problem was. And God help her, she couldn't tell him! There was no reserve of strength left in her to relive that nightmare.

"This is all about the fact that I want you out of my life."

"Are you still asking for an apology? All right, I'm sorry that I didn't try to track you down right away. I had other things, family problems, that came up and needed my attention immediately. Believe me, I wanted to find you." His arms wrapped around her, turning her to fit closely against his chest. "But you

163

were the one who ran away, my Kathleen. You're the one who decided you didn't want to be found. You left me, not the other way around."

Kathleen stiffened then took his arms from around her waist and placed them at his sides before facing him in her bitterness.

"That's right. I ran because you accused me of trying to trap you with my virginity. It didn't dawn on you that I had fallen for you in a big way, did it? That in my naivete I honestly believed what we were doing was right, not because I expected marriage or wanted to trap you, but because I thought I loved you!"

Once more his arms outstretched to capture her and still the bitter accusations that hung in the air. But she evaded him by putting the couch between them. "I tried calling you four months later, did you know?" She challenged him, her eyes sparkling with golden brown lights, her hair down and billowing over her shoulders in waves as she stood, head high, and confronted him. Her anger spilled into her hands, making them itch to slap and scratch the man in front of her for the hurt and humiliation he had put her through. Yet she also wanted him to hold her close and stroke her skin, calm her, soothe her. But the years of bitter hatred won. "I reached your brother in Florida. I tried to tell him that I needed you, that I was frightened because I was alone and pregnant and wanted your help, your love, your presence, when I had our baby. But I couldn't. I couldn't say the words. My brain screamed them into the phone, but he couldn't hear them." Tears streamed down her cheeks so they glistened. "He couldn't hear them," she repeated as she stared up at the ceiling instead of looking at the shock on Steve's face. His pain was too awful to bear. She turned around, staring into the flames again as she continued.

"Then, when I was almost six months along, I lost the baby. A beautiful baby boy. He lived for three hours. Our son died without his father even knowing that he had lived, without even caring that his son never had a chance to be held. To be loved."

"Oh, my God!" Steve voiced the anguish her revelation had brought him. "All this time and you never told me, never let me know!"

"I tried, Steve, but even your brother didn't know where you were." Her laugh was derisive. "But I paid for my mistake. And now here I am, back in the same situation and asking for the same consequences. Well, no thanks. I don't want anything else to do with you. I've worked damned hard to get where I am and nothing, especially you, is going to hurt me again."

"My God, no wonder you hated me so!" he whispered hoarsely, "All this time I couldn't understand your anger and withdrawal." His voice rasped with emotion. "I thought you were just acting, like other women I've known, harping on past mistakes and misunderstandings. I should have realized there was more to the story than I thought when I saw how your mother reacted to me, but I couldn't see anything but the need to be near you again. Your moods were driving me crazy." His lips twisted in a grimace. "And now I know the reason for them."

165

He walked around the couch, his eyes never leaving her tortured face. "I love you, Kathleen. I never would have let you suffer through that alone. You know that, don't you?"

His eyes begged her understanding, but she refused to acknowledge his hurt. "Do I? How was I supposed to know that, Steve? By the way you called me after our first encounter, when we danced all night and you held me so close? Or four weeks later, on the night you made love to me and then were furious because I wasn't promiscuous enough for your taste. That was the same night that you accused me of trying to 'catch' you, if I recall. Then the day you walked into my office you implied that I needed a man, any man, to turn me into a desirable woman. Is that your idea of 'standing by' and not letting me 'suffer' alone?"

His body went rigid at her scathing words. "Are you going to allow what happened four years ago to come between what we have now?" He took another step closer to her. "Are you trying to punish me now for what happened then?"

"Yes!" she cried, "Yes, yes, yes! I may have allowed you to make love to my body, but you'll never have any part of my heart. You're selfish, Steve, too selfish to have any sort of a relationship that would last. And as you remember, I'm not too good with the short term. So, please, if you love me as much as you say, leave me alone. Get out of my life."

Steve took another step toward her. "You're going to let the past come between us? You're going to punish us both for something that I didn't even know about until now?" He shouted in angry frustration as he attempted to reach her once more. "I don't believe it! You can't do this to us! I won't let you!"

Pain lined Steve's face and Kathleen wavered, hungry for his arms to cradle her, hold her. But a picture of little Andy swam before her eyes and her resolve quickly stiffened.

"You have no choice, Steve. Now get out." It was the quiet coldness in her voice that halted him.

The old Steve, the Steve she knew four years ago, came to the foreground in the form of a natural arrogance. His gray eyes penetrated her very being, scalding her with his intensity. Then he slowly turned, dismissing her from his very mind, and walked out the sliding doors, closing them behind him with a firm thud.

The hurting ache of four years ago was nothing compared to what Kathleen felt now. She finally had the satisfaction of telling Steve West what he had done to her years ago. She was finally able to throw his behavior back in his face, letting him know in no uncertain terms just what a louse he really was. Where was the sense of satisfaction at uncovering his sins? Where was that feeling of self-rightousness she'd expected?

All she felt was a terrible stinging loneliness that seemed to stretch monotonously ahead of her for all the years to come.

CHAPTER EIGHT

Kathleen did not see Steve during the next two days, but far off she could see Merrie riding one of the large Thoroughbred horses or taking the potential guests and customers down to the barns in one of the club's carts. She stayed as far away as she could from the people that milled about, sticking to the small brick paths that wound in and out of the trees. At night the busboy, Tim, would deliver her meals, and then quietly pick up the almost untouched tray in the morning.

Kathleen had worked hard, and now had only two more cabins to complete, and that wouldn't take more than another day. She could finish the multitude of paperwork back at the office.

Two days after her confrontation with Steve there was a tentative knock on the door and Kathleen involuntarily stiffened before brushing aside her premonition and walking calmly to open it.

Merrie stood in the doorway, her slim arms circling her body to help keep her warm. She stamped her feet, concentrating on the ground before looking up, almost afraid to see Kathleen's reaction to her presence.

"May I come in?" she questioned hesitantly. And as Kathleen silently moved aside to allow entrance, she stepped over the doorway and into the hall. "Kathleen, I'd like to talk to you, if I may."

"Surely." Kathleen walked leisurely back into the living room, curled up on the corner of the couch and watched with seeming disinterest as Merrie shed her thin cardigan sweater and warmed her hands in front of the fire. She didn't offer Merrie anything to drink, she'd only be here a few moments anyway, Kathleen imagined.

Merrie suddenly turned and confronted her new friend. Her chin rose and her eyes sparkled with determination. "Carlos confessed he told you about Andy, and your reaction. And I know you were shocked to find he isn't my late husband's child. Are you that disgusted with me?"

"Of course not, Merrie." Kathleen continued to stare into the fire. "I understand probably more than you know."

"Then why the sudden freeze?" Merrie persisted, almost willing Kathleen to look at her.

"I've been busy trying to finish up so I can leave. I need to continue with my career. This is just a short interlude."

"And then you can forget about us and live your solitary life. Once more you'll be free of friends and lovers who complicate things." Merrie's voice was so acrid that it startled Kathleen. She glanced up at the other woman, her eyes wide with surprise. "Oh, yes." Merrie nodded her head in understanding. "You want to run away and hide, just like I once did." Merrie smiled sadly. "You see, I know all the symptoms. I've been there."

"Then I'm sure you understand," Kathleen murmured. She could feel the icy cloak she was trying to wrap herself in beginning to thaw. She couldn't have that. It would only hurt again, and the penalty of that was beyond thinking about.

"No. I don't," Merrie stated emphatically. "If you hide now you may never come out of that fog you surround yourself with. You're trying to shut yourself off from life's pains. Only, when you do that, you also shut away life's joys. It's not fair to you, to me as your friend, or to Steve."

"Don't lecture me, Merrie."

Merrie ignored her blunt words as she continued. "Carlos and I are getting married tomorrow. I want you to be present for the ceremony."

Kathleen's sincerity rang in her voice. "I'm truly happy for you. He loves you and Andy very much." At the small boy's name an arrow pierced her breast before she could once again don her armor. "Congratulations."

"Will you be there? The wedding's going to take place in the lodge."

Even before she finished talking Kathleen was shaking her head. "No. Don't ask me."

"You can't hide from Steve forever. He loves you and you love him!"

"Steve loves everyone. Judith, Deborah, you, me. That's his problem, as you should know by now." Kathleen averted her eyes from Merrie to stare down at her hands. But instead of seeing clenched fingers she saw Steve's face smiling with love as he looked down at her in his arms, satiated from their lovemaking. She closed her eyes in protest, but the picture stubbornly stayed with her.

"I don't know anything of the sort! He's a damn good businessman, but he's lonely, just like the rest of us."

Kathleen stood in agitation, her hands clamped together. "Come off it, Merrie, and see him for what he is! He's a no-good philanderer, going through life two-timing every woman within reach. You, of all people, should have learned that!"

"Me?" Merrie exclaimed incredulously. "Why me? If anything, I know him to be the complete opposite from the man you're describing!" Suddenly a dawning comprehension lit Merrie's eyes. "My God, I think I see! You think he's Andy's father, don't you?" That's why you haven't seen me or come by, isn't it? You weren't disgusted, you were hurt!" She was triumphant with her discovery, especially since it was borne out in Kathleen's confused look.

"Steve isn't Andy's father. Steve's brother, Ted, is," Merrie stated quietly. "Steve helped me weather the emotional storm when Ted left me to return to

Judith. He helped me find employment away from them both. He forced me to paste my life back together and raise Andy in an environment that would be healthy for both of us. Ted knows about Andy but is too weak to do anything about it, or us. We all had to start over, only I was lucky enough to have Steve's help. For that I will always be grateful."

Kathleen sat stunned. The cloak of despair she had worn was suddenly being lifted from her shoulders to be replaced with a small bubble of joy in her heart. She had been wrong about him! Kathleen was only half-listening as Merrie continued. "You see, Carlos has known all along, but I felt that he looked down on me because of the circumstances of Andy's birth. Latin men have a tendency to be unforgiving, or so I thought." She grinned sheepishly. "So I continued to give Carlos the cold shoulder. Then, when I finally realized that Carlos really loved me, I still hesitated because I wasn't sure just how much resentment he harbored toward my child. Every time he told me how Andy needed discipline I took it as a personal insult. That is, until three days ago when Carlos told me he had discussed it with you and you said to give me time and compromise. When he vowed to do just that, I realized just how paranoid I had become. He really does like Andy, he just isn't sure how to cope with a half-grown child he's only recently been in contact with. He didn't grow with Andy like I did, yet I expected him to act like an indulgent father immediately."

"Oh, Merrie." Kathleen grasped both her hands and gave a squeeze. "I'm so happy for you. I know

Carlos loves you and Andy very much." She laughed softly. "Who could help it?"

"Beats me!" Merrie quipped, that impish look back in her eyes. Relief was there also. "So do you see now why I need you as maid of honor? Please, Kathleen," she pleaded. "It will be a very small ceremony with only a few of the staff attending. Steve has consented to be best man, as I'm sure you've guessed."

Kathleen's eyes clouded at the mention of his name. "Can I let you know later, Merrie?"

"Of course. I'll be in the office until six or seven tonight. I've got to finish up some paperwork that I've been putting off all week. Give me a buzz, will you?"

"I will," she promised, walking her friend to the door.

When Merrie had gone Kathleen once more sank into the cushions of the couch. There would be no more work done today; her mind was a miniature whirlwind as she tried to absorb all that Merrie had confided.

Sometime during the day her mother called, her small birdlike voice chirping in happiness. Taylor had proposed and her mother had accepted. They would be married in a small ceremony in two weeks time. Wasn't it wonderful? Yes, it was, Kathleen said before hanging up the phone and taking a good look at the future. Wasn't she lucky? When her mother married and left, she could go home to an empty house for the rest of her life. Pride could keep her company on lonely nights, make love to her, tease her out of bad moods. Pride had a lot to answer for.

Night enfolded Kathleen's cottage before she moved from her corner of the couch. Stiff muscles cried out to be stretched. Grabbing her jacket she quickly left the cottage behind and began to wander the small brick paths, not caring which direction she was headed as long as it gave her something to do.

Although Merrie's conversation had given her hope momentarily, Kathleen couldn't help but remember and relive her own heartbreaking time four years ago. She had left the campus as quickly as humanly possible, wanting to break the frightening bond that held her to a man she hardly knew. It had been a new and terrifying experience for her, surfacing deep emotions she had never known she was capable of—a long-buried need to belong to someone emotionally, and a blatant sensuality that stunned her with its power.

Then she had realized she was pregnant and that thought terrified her even more. In her old circle of wealthy but traditionalist friends it wasn't done. Oh, movie actresses and jet-setters had children out of wedlock, but she wasn't in that sphere of sophistication. Then there was her mother, who had tried for so long and so hard to ensure that her child wouldn't suffer for the sins of the father. Would Kathleen's child suffer from not knowing his father at all? Would he or she be disillusioned at knowing the type of man his father was? Questions, questions, turning over in her mind night and day, and still she delayed the inevitable problem of telling her mother.

But that one night, when she had called Steve's home only to reach his brother, had been the final blow. All her childish hopes and dreams of discovering that he loved her and wanted both her and their child were wiped out by one bitter voice. Her mother had found her slumped over the phone, her shoulders shaking with sobs that wrenched her soul. But they had pulled together, overcoming her misery and shame, and soon the world righted itself. If life was not wonderful for Kathleen, at least it was bearable.

Four months later the child was gone. She had awakened in the middle of the night with pains that wrapped around her spine to squeeze the breath from her. She delivered a small replica of Steve, a boy three months premature and too small to live, despite the doctor's expertise. Thus ended all problems but one—how to keep her mind from dwelling on the child she had silently clung to in love and now no longer had.

That was the turning point, for her love for Steve had truly turned to hate. It had been a survival tactic. She realized that now. And yet Steve had never had the chance to say yes or no to her request of marriage for the sake of their child. She had never tried to get hold of him other than the one night she had spoken to his brother.

She continued to amble through the dark woods, her feet scuffing the small banks of snow, her head buried in the deep cowl of her sweater.

She wasn't able to bury the memory of him and the fatal fascination he had held for her four years ago.

And she couldn't do so now. She had loved him then and loved him even more now.

She knew what she had to do. She must stop running and face him, tell him what he meant to her. He was right; she was punishing both of them for something that was better left in the past. Nothing could change yesterday's circumstances, but she could change all the tomorrows.

Kathleen's steps quickened with intention as she turned toward the lodge. Above the lodge were VIP guest rooms . . . and Steve's apartment. As she drew closer she could see a light in his living room and her heart sang, her steps quickened to reach him. She almost ran through the darkened and now deserted lobby toward the elevator in her hurry to reach and tell him how she felt. Nothing was as important as seeing him. Nothing.

She pushed the third floor button, impatient for it to reach its destination. She didn't know what she would say yet . . . she'd worry about that when she reached him.

Her knock on his door was staccato quick. Her cheeks and lips were still red from the cold outside and her eyes were bright with anticipation. But when the door opened she almost lost her nerve.

"Well, well. If it isn't the angel of righteousness!" Steve was visibly irate at the interruption. He turned and walked back into the living room, taking for granted that she would follow him, apparently not caring if she left.

She closed the door and followed him.

"I need to talk to you." She walked down the

entrance hallway and into a huge room dominated by a fireplace. Steve stood by the fire, his hands wrapped around a large crystal brandy snifter, his look forbidding. Jeans hugged the muscles of his thighs and a wine-colored velour shirt tightened around his biceps and slim hips, opening at the neck to show the growth of hair that matted his chest in dark golden curls.

"What the hell do you want?" he growled, his husky voice slightly slurred. "Why don't you just leave the way you came? I don't feel like listening to more of your insults."

"I won't leave until I talk to you, Steve." Her voice sounded calm and businesslike. No one would have ever known she was shaking like an aspen leaf under his scrutiny.

His dark gray eyes never left Kathleen's as he reached over and flicked off the lamplight closest to him, putting his face in shadow.

"Say what you have to say, Kathleen, and make it quick. As you can see I've made other plans for the evening." His mouth turned up in a sneer as he lifted his drink in salute before gulping another mouthful. His words hurt, but she wouldn't let that stop her. Not now.

"I love you, Steve."

"Bravo," he drawled. "Me and how many others?" Before she could answer he continued. "What a great little actress you've turned out to be. The maiden with dubious morals loves only me." He laughed. "Deborah could probably get you into the movies if she wanted to. Only she wouldn't. One tramp never helps another."

"At least you see her for what she is."

"Deborah never makes a pretense. She is what she is and people accept her for herself. Others try to hide behind transparent covers, proclaiming innocence, shifting tons of guilt to others, when all the time they're just as bad. At least Deborah is honest."

The words stung like a sharp hand across her face. She hadn't been honest about her feelings, but she had never been lax in morals either. How could she protest the one accusation without him accepting the other? Suddenly she knew the overwhelming taste of defeat. He would never believe her now.

His hoarse voice cut into her thoughts. "And what makes you believe in this great love now? Where was it earlier? You know you always withheld a part of yourself from me." He shook his head, not waiting for an answer. "Well, thanks for the thought, but I don't need your love anymore, shallow as it is. Give it to someone who's willing to pay the emotional price for it. I'm sure you won't have any problem . . ." His gray eyes raked her slim body. "At least you have all the equipment in the right places."

Her head jerked up to stare at him, involuntarily responding to his venom. Gray shadows played upon the planes of his face and she couldn't quite see the hatred that must have been apparent in his eyes.

She stood straight, tears cascading down her cheeks to run unchecked. She refused to hide them from him. "I wasn't asking for anything from you, Steve. I just wanted you to know. I was silly enough to hope it would make a difference." She halted, her voice cracking slightly. She cleared her throat, her brown eyes glistening as she devoured his lean, taut features for the last time. "Good-bye," she stated quietly.

She walked to the door and stopped just short of closing it, totally humbled at the amount of bitterness she had evoked. It was her punishment for being so very quick to accuse in the first place. She deserved his anger after her tirade.

Suddenly she stopped. Yes, she deserved his anger, but she didn't deserve to lose him. Hadn't he said he loved her, and didn't she just admit the same to him?

But instead of her anger waning, it waxed brighter. The nerve of him! He was trying to punish her! Well, she'd show him that the Boltons were made of stronger stuff. Ben used to say that the best defense was a good offense, and that's exactly what she planned to do. She would attack first and destroy any notions he might have had before he even had a chance! She openly grinned at the thought.

She cooled her temper down to a thinking point by walking the hallway for a while. Then, having thought out what she would say that would thaw him the quickest, she walked with determined purpose toward the living room, her eyes alive with the light of battle.

Steve was standing much as she had left him, a brandy in his hand as he watched the fire play upon the hearth. When he heard her step he looked up expectantly before shuttered lids hid the emotions deep inside. But for one split-second she had seen the look of hunger there.

"Back again, Miss Bolton?" His voice was low and silky, but because she sensed he was expecting her to give way to a tirade, she didn't.

She couldn't help staring at him. Although her mind tried to control her body movements, she still watched as if famished. His every move, his every nuance made her want to hold him close, comfort him, make love to him.

"And how can I help you, Miss Bolton?" he inquired politely, but there was a sheepish smile tugging at his deep dimples. A smile! Where was his anger, his indignant insults? Where was the coldness that he had shown her just five minutes ago? Damn him! Was he playing some game she didn't know the rules to again?

"Oh, my Kathleen! I love you." He walked toward her slowly, his arms outstretched to enfold her.

She stared at him. Her golden-brown eyes flickered, attempting to fathom his methods. Somehow this wasn't going as planned.

Steve shook his head again, a small, tender and slightly sheepish smile glowing in his eyes. "No, darling. You're not insane. You just had a few minutes to think about us and came up with a change of heart . . . and so did I. I was frustrated because I couldn't have the very thing I wanted most. Then you offered it to me and I was so down because you had already refused that I forgot my goal: you. You're staying here with me."

"I didn't—" She cleared her throat, her eyes darting frantically around the room for an escape. There was none. "I didn't have a change of heart at all," she lied. "I just decided that you should accept my apology now instead of making us both wait for something we both want." At his intense look a tingling warmth was invading her senses. Questions turned topsy-turvy in her head, but she couldn't coordinate her brain and mouth to move at the same time.

"You're absolutely right. I want you too much to argue over who was hurt and who was right." He held out his arms, opening them for her to come close to his body.

"I've planned this for too long to be crazy, darling. Ever since I found out from your old roommate, Sandy, where you were, I've been scheming for a way to get you here." Kathleen stared at him, open-mouthed, as he continued. "Our wires were crossed and too many things and people got in the way the last time you came and went in my life. So for the past year I've been biding my time, waiting for a chance to call on you in such a way that you would have no retreat. I finally found one, and here you are."

Tears stung her eyes at the loving tenderness of his expression.

His arms finally encircled her, his hand cupping her head to rest against his chest. His hand stroked the silkiness of her hair.

"I can't believe you really love me," she murmured against his chest, her mind still reeling with the wonder of it all.

He gave her a light squeeze as he sighed heavily. "You'd better, you little witch. You've kept me awake more nights than I'd care to admit. I've got to marry you just so I can catch up on my sleep." His chest rumbled with a chuckle. His hand tilted her face up toward him and he stared deeply into her eyes, silently telling her things she never would have believed possible.

"I love you so much, my Kathleen," he murmured before his lips claimed hers in total possession, and her heart swelled in capitulation. She was his, and there was no way she could tell herself otherwise. His tongue ravaged her mouth in his urgency to take her love. His hands traveled constantly, wandering from her hips to her breasts, a low moan echoing deep in his throat. Reluctantly he gave a deep sigh and pushed her back from him, still retaining a firm possessive hold on her waist. He stared down at her with a look that spoke of tenderness and love and her heart was filled to overflowing.

"I need you." His voice broke with emotion. In a moment she was back in his arms, enfolded in his own possessive nest of security. She was home. Anywhere he was, was home for her. It was a shame it had taken her so long to find that out.

His mouth came down to invade her very being with his kisses. Her eyes closed languorously. She leaned against him, her hands clutching the strength of his broad shoulders. His mouth trailed away from hers, seeking the softness just behind her ear, the hollow at the base of her throat, the soft throbbing at her temples. His fingers twisted through the silkiness of her hair as he once more found the soft moistness of her ready mouth.

She was chilled, then a heat would sear her skin, then once again she would shiver in delight.

Without words he led her to the couch, his fingers impatient with her securely buttoned blouse. She helped him, then reached to undo his belt as she watched his face flush with wanting.

Only seconds passed and they were naked, lying in each other's arms. Steve's hands drifted up her sides to gently stroke her breasts, his tongue on her slightly salted skin making her nerve endings dance an ancient tune. Her body yielded naturally to fit the curves and contours of his hardened muscles as they moved together in preparation for the ultimate act of togetherness and love.

Deft fingers found the lean ridges of his chest and stomach, her nails teasing his flesh further by cupping his muscular buttocks and bringing him as close as flesh would allow.

They made love with an intensity that would imprint itself on their memory for years to come.

Later, much later, Steve held her close to him as they stretched out on the couch in the late night. His arm cradled her head, his hand still absently stroking the softness of her limbs.

"Choose a day of the week you want to get married," he muttered into her ear, stopping his nibbling only as long as it took to speak the words.

"But you don't have to marry me, Steve. You never did," she stated softly, caressing the strength of his jaw.

"Oh, yes I do. That's all I ever wanted to do, but you were like a striking virago one moment and a shy, hunted doe the next. I was afraid to broach the subject for fear you'd flee and I would have to find you again. I thought if I were patient and gave you more time to know me, you'd be willing to become Mrs. West." He gave her forehead a chaste kiss, his lips warm and firm against her still heated flesh. "I've spent four years trying to get the opportunity to tell you that, without worrying whether you would slip out of my arms and disappear again."

She chuckled. "Don't tell me you weren't busy with other women, Steve. You've kept in practice." She tried to pass the others in his life off casually, but her eyes begged an honest answer.

His face was solemn, as if a cloud had passed over to shadow him. "No. I won't lie, darling. After you ran out on me that night so long ago I tried to forget you. No one seemed to know where you were. You don't know how much I regretted my anger with you. My only excuse was that I had never met anyone like you before and when I found I was the first, I was shocked. I didn't understand your giving me such a gift with no strings attached." His fingers memorized her face as he continued almost absently, as if he were thinking aloud. "Then I was so busy with my family and the business. I kept thinking of you and getting angry, then frustrated, telling myself that no one woman should be able to get under my skin like you did. I finally thought I had gotten over you until my little sister mentioned that she had seen Sandy, your old roommate, and she had said you were doing well. I called her up and caught up with you." His hands tightened. "The polo center was almost completed and I decided it was time to confront you. I wanted to see if you still affected me the same way or if I had dreamed you up and it was all an illusion with no substance between us." He grinned reminiscently, twisting her heart. "But the magic was still present, as if there had been no time apart. Only you were so feisty, so hard to reach."

"I was frightened." Her voice cracked into the warmth of his chest.

He chuckled. "You certainly didn't act like it! You almost tore me limb from limb! I knew I had a fight on my hands to get you back, but the moment I saw you again I knew I wanted you like I wanted nothing else in my life."

"What about Judith?" Her voice sounded far away, muffled in his chest.

"Judith was my second crush." He grinned, unrepentant. "My first was my fourth-grade teacher." His voice lowered. "And you're my last. I'm old enough now to know my own true love."

"And Deborah?"

"She owns a film company. She wants to do a movie here." The silence was deafening. She needed to know more and he was reluctant to tell her.

She peeped at him, only to find him staring gravely at her. His hand came down and forced her to look deeply into his eyes once more. "I used Deborah just as I've used many women over the years, my Kathleen. I wish I could say otherwise. But none of them have meant very much to me. With you, my darling,

185

I'll never need another woman, and I certainly don't want any other. You're enough to satisfy me for the rest of my days."

She gave a sigh. She couldn't bury the memory and fatal fascination of him four years ago. Now she knew there was no turning back. She had loved him then, and she loved him even more so now.

His touch was tender, almost reverent, as his thumb followed the delicate arch of her brows to her high cheekbones to follow the line down to her lips. His finger pressed softly and she parted them, taking his finger and sucking gently, her tongue wrapping delicately around his nail. His breath hissed in his throat, eyes turning a stormy black. There were still things that needed explaining, but later. Much later.

Her eyes lit with mischief mixed with a hint of seduction that sparkled under her half-closed lids. "And what are we doing in the middle of the living room? Why aren't we in bed celebrating our wedding to come?"

His expression was one of total surprise before he gave her a quick hug. He chuckled again. "That's what I mean, my Kathleen. No one else is as devilish as you are." He lifted a brow, leering intentionally. "And if we had time, I'd take you in that room and do all the things I ever dreamed of doing. But Merrie and Carlos are getting married this morning and we're supposed to be there."

She took his hand, her fingers twining with his, and began leading him toward the door she knew was the bedroom. "And you don't think we have enough time? Come on. Besides, the wedding can't start without us, can it?"

His eyes narrowed, his hand tightening in hers. "No. They can't start without us." His voice was like warm velvet against her nerves.

"And this time, Steve West, I get to dress and undress you. I always wondered how it would be to peel away the clothes of a business tycoon, if only to find what's underneath," she teased throatily.

"My darling, you're in for a surprise. Each tycoon is different. Not that you will ever have the opportunity to find out. Ever," he murmured, before pulling her back into his arms, picking her up, and placing her on the bed.

Perhaps he was right. Each tycoon was different. But this one was totally hers. And that's all that mattered.

LOOK FOR NEXT MONTH'S
CANDLELIGHT ECSTASY ROMANCES ®

Dell Bestsellers

- ☐ **ELIZABETH TAYLOR: The Last Star**
  by Kitty Kelley...**$3.95** (12410-7)

- ☐ **THE LEGACY** by Howard Fast....................**$3.95** (14719-0)

- ☐ **LUCIANO'S LUCK** by Jack Higgins...........**$3.50** (14321-7)

- ☐ **MAZES AND MONSTERS** by Rona Jaffe...**$3.50** (15699-8)

- ☐ **TRIPLETS** by Joyce Rebeta-Burditt...........**$3.95** (18943-8)

- ☐ **BABY** by Robert Lieberman.......................**$3.50** (10432-7)

- ☐ **CIRCLES OF TIME** by Phillip Rock.............**$3.50** (11320-2)

- ☐ **SWEET WILD WIND** by Joyce Verrette......**$3.95** (17634-4)

- ☐ **BREAD UPON THE WATERS**
  by Irwin Shaw..**$3.95** (10845-4)

- ☐ **STILL MISSING** by Beth Gutcheon............**$3.50** (17864-9)

- ☐ **NOBLE HOUSE** by James Clavell...............**$5.95** (16483-4)

- ☐ **THE BLUE AND THE GRAY**
  by John Leekley..**$3.50** (10631-1)

Desert Hostage

Diane Dunaway

Behind her is England and her first innocent encounter
with love. Before her is a mysterious land of forbidding
majesty. Kidnapped, swept across the deserts of
Araby, Juliette Barclay sees her past vanish in the
endless, shifting sands. Desperate and defiant, she
seeks escape only to find harrowing danger, to
discover her one hope in the arms of her captor, the
Shiek of El Abadan. Fearless and proud, he alone can
tame her. She alone can possess his soul. Between
them lies the secret that will bind her to him forever, a
woman possessed, a slave of love.

A DELL BOOK   11963-4 $3.95

A woman's place—the parlor, not the concert stage! But radiant Diana Ballantyne, pianist extraordinaire, had one year before she would bow to her father's wishes, return to England and marry. She had given her word, yet the moment she met the brilliant Maestro, Baron Lukas von Korda, her fate was sealed. He touched her soul with music, kissed her lips with fire, filled her with unnameable desire. One minute warm and passionate, the next aloof, he mystified her, tantalized her. She longed for artistic triumph, ached for surrender, her passions ignited by Vienna dreams.

A DELL BOOK 19530-6 $3.50

Vienna Dreams

by JANETTE RADCLIFFE